# LASHAWN VASSER

# REMINGTON'S
## Sky

# REMINGTON'S SKY

# By

# LaShawn Vasser

**Join Author LaShawn Vasser's newsletter for Advanced Reader Copies, Giveaways, and Information regarding upcoming releases. PLEASE JOIN HERE.**

persons living or dead are entirely coincidental.
All rights reserved.

**\*EXPLICIT ADULT CONTENT\***
**WARNING**

This novel is considered romantic fiction with erotic elements or erotica. This is for mature audiences only. This book contains profane adult language, mild violence, and strong sexual content.

# Dedications & Acknowledgments

THANK YOU to all of the readers who have come along with me on this incredible journey!

**You guys the ROCK!**

# Prologue

"It's not safe."

"You won't change my mind." Charlie Kneeland was defiant.

"Why are you so stubborn?  You can't go sneaking around in the wee hours of the morning by yourself."  Yolanda whisper-yelled, as her eyes flitted from the open bedroom door to Charlie.  It was obvious her words were falling on deaf ears.  *Her* being Yolanda Garcia, the daughter of Charlie's mother's live-in house manager.  Yolanda also sometimes doubled as Charlie's best-friend and pretend older sibling—although only by two years.

*How ironic*, Charlie thought, glancing around at her bubble-gum pink walls, the extra-large canopy bed draped in white lace with the fluffy pink and white comforter to match. A *room fit for a princess.*  She smiled sadly. Her dolls sat on the shelves, watching her every move.  They had seen it all. Fortunately, *this time* Charlie's absolute favorite toy, La La, was face down and placed innocently in the center of her bed unable to take in the scene.

While it was true her room had all the frills meant for a princess, there was just one problem—*Charlie wasn't a princess*.

To an outsider, she had way more things than she needed.  Charlie knew it was true.  She would probably have appreciated her room more if the décor hadn't been about a magazine shoot to gin up publicity for her mom's movie. It had nothing to do with her.  And those people, those outsiders, never had to witness the horrors that had occurred in her room

i

over the past few years.  So, to the unsuspecting person, it was every little girl's dream.  Angrily, Charlie brought a cigarette up to her lips and lit it.

She hated her room.  She hated everything about it.  "Can you open my bay windows?  It's a beautiful night.  I love the way the moon shines in through it."

Yolanda ignored her.  "So, you're smoking now!?  It's not even the vapor kind.  You're only twelve, Charlie.  Those things are going to for sure give you cancer."

Charlie shrugged and pushed herself off the door.  She walked over and pushed the windows open herself.  They were large, more like French doors than windows.  "I'm glad you're concerned, but it's not necessary.  I can take care of myself.  I have been doing it for a long time."

Yolanda stomped over to Charlie and got in her face.  "Not if you're smoking, knowing it's bad for you."  Yolanda snatched the little white stick out of Charlie's tiny hand and stalked away.  The next thing Charlie heard was the toilet flush.  Yolanda had disposed of it.  "What is wrong with you?  Is this why you got kicked out of school earlier this week? For smoking?"

Charlie fell back onto her bed.  Her long, glossy blonde hair fanned out over it.  She stared up at her canopy and reached for La La.  She held the doll tight to her chest.  "No.  I got kicked out of school because they found alcohol in my things."

"Charlie!  You're smoking and drinking too?  What kind of school is this?  I thought it was one of the best."

"It is.  The best money can buy, and that includes drugs and alcohol."

"This is so unlike you.  Ma Ma says your grades are falling too.  I don't understand.  What's going on?"  Disappointed, Yolanda sat down next to her.  It was then she noticed that Charlie's eyes had closed and tears were leaking down the sides.

"It wasn't mine.  I don't drink or do drugs.  I don't know who put it there, but I'm glad.  I hated that place.  The problem is—I hate this place too."

"You don't mean that.  But I have to be honest.  I never understood why your parents sent you to that school anyway?"

Charlie lifted her head off the mattress and cracked one eye open. "Other than the obvious?"

"What do you mean?"

"My family is not like yours.  Your parents actually like you.  My mom and dad are too busy to know I even exist.  But, to answer your question, I caught Kane cheating on my mom with her assistant.  Showed her the pictures and everything.  Next thing I knew, I was being shipped off to a boarding school.  I should have sent the nudies to that gossip rag, TNZ, instead."

Yolanda's eyes grew large in surprise.  "You're kidding?  Your mom's husband was cheating with her assistant?"

"Yep."  Charlie popped the *p* at the end of the word so hard that it reverberated around the room.  "She won't divorce him because of *appearances* and all."

"Why didn't she just send you to your dad's?"

In a voice, dead of emotion, Charlie answered, "Child support."

"No way. There's got to be more. Your mom's already rich, and so is Kane."

"No. There isn't any more to it than that and looks can be very deceiving. They are broke. An aging actress just doesn't command the same kind of payday that she used to and certainly not one that would keep her living as lavishly as she does without my dad's money. I overheard her accountant say something about curbing her spending. It costs almost a hundred thousand a month just for lawn care and maintenance for our estate. My dad pays for it, but she's cutting costs and pocketing the savings."

Yolanda's mouth dropped. "Whoa. That's more than my mom makes in a year."

Charlie sat propped up on her elbows. She felt bad for complaining. Charlie wasn't a stupid girl. She knew that even on her worst day, as far as money, they had it better than most. "Well, remember, my mom hasn't been in a movie in three years. And Kane . . ." Charlie rolled her eyes. "Nobody really knows what he does. I guess he just screws assistants and spends my dad's money." Her voice dropped, and the sadness in it was palpable. "They deserve each other."

Yolanda felt sorry for Charlie. "You don't mean that." She reached out to place a soothing hand on Charlie's shoulder.

Charlie winced and jerked her body away.  Her voice was strained with pain.  "Yes.  I do."

Concern was evident on Yolanda's face.  "What's wrong?"

Charlie debated being honest for just a second then decided to tell the truth.  She could show Yolanda better than tell her.  Charlie lifted her t-shirt to reveal yellowish, purple and blue marks all over her ribcage and parts of her back and shoulder.

Horrified, Yolanda began speaking in Spanish.  "What in the world?  What happened to you?"

"Courtesy of Kane for being disobedient and looking at him with defiance in my eyes."

"H-he hit you?" Yolanda was shocked.  "You've got to tell your mom."

Charlie nodded.  "She knows.  It's not the first time, the second, or the third.  That's why I'm getting out of here before I'm punished for getting kicked out of school.  When really I'm being punished for being Remington Kneeland's daughter."

"I didn't know."

"Nobody does except for my mom."

"Does he hit her too?"

"Not that I am aware of.  I think I'm the only one who wins that lottery."

Yolanda couldn't believe that the famous *Bella Lord-Kneeland,* now, *Bella Lord-Langston* would allow such a thing to happen to her child. While she didn't support Charlie's decision to run away, Yolanda fully understood why she would want to leave. "How are you going to get past security? Someone is always at the front gate."

"I'm not going through the gate. I'm going to sneak out the south part of the estate by the service entrance next to the stables. There is a new security guard there. He falls asleep like clockwork around 1:30 a.m."

"How do you know that?"

"I heard the head of security warning him about it. I need to make my escape before he gets fired."

"Where will you go?"

"I've got a couple thousand dollars saved. I'll figure it out once I'm out of here. Maybe I can try to stay with my old math tutor. She was nice."

"I don't know, Charlie." Yolanda was more than a bit skeptical. "I still think you should tell your dad. You're not even old enough to rent a hotel room." Yolanda could see that Charlie was about to protest. "Okay. Okay." She put her palms out. "At least, tell my mom."

"First, my dad's in China. He's almost never around anymore. And, even if he was, what's he going to do? *Nothing.* My mom has great lawyers. Your mom works for my mom. If you tell her, how is that going to work? I'll tell you how. It won't. Ms. Sophia would get fired, and I can't put your mom in that position. And for future reference, you would be surprised at what an extra hundred dollars can convince people to do. You've got to promise me that you'll keep quiet about this."  Charlie needed to make sure Yolanda understood.  She pleaded.  "You've seen my bruises.  Next time, Kane might kill me."

At her words, Yolanda's head snapped up. She stared into Charlie's eyes, which revealed the real fear Charlie felt.  Against her better judgement, Yolanda gave in.  "I'll keep quiet but only if you promise to text and keep me updated about where you are."

Visibly relieved, Charlie whispered, "I promise."

Careful not to put too much pressure on Charlie's injuries, Yolanda reached out and pulled her friend into a much-needed hug.

# Chapter 1

*Not this shit again.*

Inwardly, Sky cringed as her eyeballs rolled into the back of her head while she sipped on a glass of red wine. Fortunately, Nia couldn't see her face. The woman was, seemingly, looking straight ahead and staring out into space.

Sky was sympathetic to her plight . . . *to a point.* Only, this exact situation had played out so many times before, kind of like *Groundhog Day,* over and over again. So, after witnessing this same routine in the past, the moment Nia phoned about needing to get together, Sky knew exactly how her evening was going to go down.

It wasn't the words Nia had spoken during the call, but the tone that told the story. Sky had become very familiar with it and knew *what* as well as *who* had caused the changes in Nia's mood and *why.*

*That fool had had another affair.* Only this time, it was with a different woman.

As irritated as Sky had been about Nia continuing to endure the cycle of insanity, she was still her best friend. There would come a moment to be brutally honest for the millionth and one time, but this wasn't it. For now, she would drink like a sailor so that she could continue to listen and comfort, not rub salt in Nia's wounds with *I told you sos.*

Sky sat quietly with her feet curled up on the sofa watching Nia, who was on the other end of the couch, bawling her eyes out over Steven's latest

1

betrayal. Even though Sky had convinced herself to remain mum, she imagined reaching over, grabbing Nia by the shoulders, and shaking the shit out of her while screaming *GET THE HELL OFF THE CRAZY TRAIN*! Again, though, she wouldn't, not today. Instead, Sky would calmly sip her drink. It kept her from acting out and spewing the words that were on the tip of her tongue.

Tears streamed down Nia's face. Her nose was raw and red as she sniffed uncontrollably. Mechanically, Sky grabbed a tissue out of the box that sat between them and handed one over.

"Why can't the man be faithful?" *Sniff. Sniff.* "He promised he wouldn't do this again." Nia wiped the tears from her eyes and blew her nose.

*Because he's a hoe.* Another sip was in order as Sky mused. *And it's not again . . .* It's *again and again and again.*

To keep herself quiet, Sky brought the glass to her lips and took another long swallow. Still, it wasn't enough to keep her mouth in check, so Sky took another drink. As the dark liquid meandered down her throat, it left her feeling warm all over. Sky allowed her eyes to drift closed as she savored the tangy plum flavor and swirled the fruity taste around with her tongue. A good wine always took her to a magical place. It was impossible to blurt out the obvious with a mouth full of merlot. Her mind was awhirl with thoughts, and by the miracle of alcohol, none of them made it past her lips, *not yet.*

Sky could hear the steady tone of Nia's voice, but somehow, managed to block out the words and briefly tuned her out. Although Sky's subconscious was trying to get a million miles away, her conscious mind wouldn't allow it. Instead, Sky slowly opened her eyes and sat stoically in the darkness. She was enraptured by the golden glow from the fireplace as it illuminated the room. Her movements were slow and deliberate as she lifted her glass to study it. *I could have sworn it was full just a moment ago*? It was a good thing that Nia was talking mostly to herself and wasn't really expecting a response. Sky wasn't paying close enough attention and didn't know what the hell she had been talking about.

"What do you think I should do? Steven keeps calling me." Nia's words finally broke through Sky's fog of thoughts. She stared at her cell phone as the tears continued to fall down her face. "He probably won't stop unless I answer It. At the very minimum, I should cuss his ass out."

"Mmhmm." Sky nodded slightly. She had been dreading the "what should I do?" question and hoped her non-answer was enough to pacify Nia, since she hadn't been able to get the woman drunk enough to pass out before she asked it. Nia didn't honestly want to hear how Sky really felt. So, Sky pretended as if she hadn't heard her while continuing to examine her glass. *It was much too low for this conversation.* Sky peered over into Nia's glass and realized hers was too. *Perfect time for a refill.* "I think we could use just a little more wine." Sky leaned over toward the coffee table to pick up the almost empty bottle. For anyone counting, it was their third. Typically, Sky would never encourage drinking to deal with a problematic issue. As a doctor, she knew better, but this was more for her than Nia. Sky was doing her best to keep from saying something hurtful. This conversation was one they had had before, and unfortunately, it had led to them not speaking for almost a month.  Sky was mindful of that.

"Seriously?  What would you do?"  Nia wouldn't let it go.  Her swollen face and red-rimmed eyes were filled with pain and desperation.

"Before or after I cut off his balls and shove them down that woman's throat?"  *Did I say that out loud, or did I think it*?  Sky wasn't sure, but by the look on Nia's face, she'd spoken them aloud.  *Maybe this is not a good time for me to be more than a little tipsy, without a mouthful of wine.*

"That's a felony.  You and I would never risk our licenses by doing something like that."

Sky wasn't so sure.  She shrugged.  "Well, you did burn all of his clothes.  Last I checked, that was illegal too.  I figure, if we're going to lose our licenses, I would want to do something a little more lasting and memorable."

"Burning clothes is a misdemeanor.  Anyway, I couldn't catch her.  She ran out of the apartment before I could get my hands on her." Nia threw her head back against the sofa.  "Steven said he knows he has a problem and that he loves me enough to get therapy."

*Like a sex addict?*  Sky knew they existed, but that wasn't Steven's problem.  He was just a selfish pig.  *Was Nia really starting to buy into his bullshit after less than twenty-four hours?*  How many times did the man have to cheat before Nia understood Steven would never change?  Some things just happened like clockwork—*The sun rose in the east and water was*

4

*wet.* Those things were facts and were not changing, and neither was Steven.

"Are you serious?" Sky's voice was more angry than shocked.

Nia kept talking. "He's never been willing to try therapy. Sex addiction is real."

Sky responded. "So is the bubonic plague. Both of them can kill you."

Nia didn't hear her as she glanced down at her phone and briefly closed her eyes. "He's calling again."

"If you don't want to talk to him, turn off the phone." *Easy enough for a person who really doesn't want to be bothered.* "And I was serious about physical bodily harm. Considering I'm a doctor, I could have come up with a great medical excuse for why Steven didn't need his man parts and why they found their way into that woman's esophagus. You're a lawyer. You're smart enough to figure out the legal reason to justify it. If an attorney can get a privileged white kid off for murder due to that made up affluenza defense, we certainly could come up with an excuse way more creative and convincing than that."

Nia lifted her head slightly and turned sad eyes toward Sky. "No matter how much money you or I make, with our brown skin, we would never get away with an affluenza-like defense. They would lock us up and throw away the key." Nia sighed.

Sky swirled her wine around in her glass. "If you say so. I still think it is worth a try."

"You *were* kidding right?" Sometimes, Nia couldn't tell if Sky was serious or not.

Sky didn't blink or crack a smile. Her void-of-emotions resting face, or as Nia like to call it—*the disguise*—usually hid what Sky was feeling.

Slow to respond, Nia answered for her. "I know you didn't really mean that." At least, Nia hoped she didn't. "Anyway, I've told you, I wouldn't make a good inmate. I'm not cozying up to Big Bertha for protection."

Sky licked her lips and simply stated, "Okay." Then drained the rest of her drink.

Nervously, Nia laughed. "I-I'm going to just chalk that suggestion up to the wine talking."

Sky placed her glass down on the table. She couldn't hold it in any longer. "If you must. But look, since we're both almost drunk, don't hold my words against me in the morning. Steven's only problem is that he's a jerk. He was a cheating scumbag when we were in college, and he still is. I don't think he's ever going to change. I've seen him belittle you and tear down your self-confidence. You have too much going for yourself to continually put up with his crap. Give yourself a chance to be appreciated by someone else. Hell, give another guy a chance to screw up. If you're not going to do that or commit to choking him to death for your own sanity, change your number, the locks to your doors, and forget about him."

Fresh tears rolled down Nia's cheeks. She whispered, "Sky . . . I'm not like you. I want love in my life. I love being in love. I can't just shut off my emotions."

Sky scrunched up her face as if tasting something sour. *What was she talking about?* Sky wanted to find real love too, and she didn't turn off her emotions. Just because she didn't let them rule her and wasn't so quick to give her heart to undeserving assholes didn't mean she didn't want love. "I have feelings *and* standards. You should try it. I've heard it's sexy."

Nia began to rationalize her situation. "Look, you've never really been in love or in a long-term relationship since college. I know you're dating Noah, but I can't honestly tell how you feel about him. In relationships, there is give and take. You don't just cut someone off because they make mistakes, which is what you do all the time. I know Steven is a hot mess, but he's *my* hot mess. It's not like there are that many eligible black men around. So, I understand how he can be tempted by women throwing themselves at him."

Nia's words stung and pissed Sky off. Sky couldn't help herself. "Oh, my god. Are you really buying into the endangered black man myth? Men are like a pair of shoes. They are everywhere! You can get a good or bad pair. I don't wear anything that makes my feet hurt. I prefer Jimmy Choos not bargain basement or thrift store specials. And, for the record, Steven's not just your hot mess but hers too."

Pissed, Nia sat up straight. "He said they were only together once!"

"One time is too many!"

7

The fight went out of Nia as she sagged back into the couch. "I don't know if I want to give up on our relationship. I know you can't stand Steven, but he has some amazing qualities. And let's not forget, I've invested too many years to give up and start over. I want a family. I'm not getting any younger. If therapy can work, maybe I should at least give it a try. You might be fine growing older alone, but I'm not."

*Growing older with Steven? That was never going to happen. And family . . .* That entire concept was foreign to Sky. Her parents divorced when she was a young child. Still, hearing those words come from the one person whose relationship she valued more than any other was painful.

Sky knew that people thought she was cold and calculating, but she'd had to be. Otherwise, the world would have swallowed her up, and she would never have reached this level of success, especially if she had to depend on *feelings*.

Nia leaned over and placed her head on Sky's shoulder. "I'm sorry. I didn't mean that. I'm devastated, and it's the wine talking."

They sat silently for a while both pondering each other's words until Nia's breathing started to even out. *Now she passes out. Murphy's Law.*

Sky glanced down at her friend. She loved Nia like a sister, and she didn't deserve Steven's asshattery. Her heart was just too soft and too forgiving when it came to him. Sky readily admitted her heart was mostly made of stone—*too many disappointments*. Sky continued to compare herself to Nia. She was much better off. Silly emotions are what had Nia tied up in knots, and Steven had her mind so twisted, the woman didn't know if she were coming or going.

In her sleep, Nia clutched her wine glass in one hand and her cell phone in the other. Sky removed the glass and sat it on the table next to the now empty bottle of merlot. Just like clockwork, as it had all night, her cell phone vibrated. It had been a symphony of buzzing noises and was still vibrating at almost three o'clock in the morning. Sky half expected Nia to jump up out of her sleep to answer it, but she hadn't. Nia had evidently fallen into a wine-induced sleep-like coma. After a second, or two, when she still didn't move, Sky gently removed the phone from her hands and looked at the screen. Just as she had suspected, the number on the display was Steven's.

Sky shut off her phone, and as she stood with it in hand, the room tilted. Sky stood stock still. Once she felt as if her feet were on solid ground, Sky reached to grab the afghan that was draped over the back of her sofa and placed it on to Nia's sleeping form.

"*Ugh.* We made a mess." Sky didn't want to wake up to that in the morning. So, she decided to clean up a little. "Whoa." She must have moved too fast because the room started to spin again. Sky stilled and extended her arms out to steady herself. After a couple of moments, it did. Carefully, she bent down to pick up their wine glasses. Sky stumbled into the kitchen, and placed Nia's phone on the island, then tossed the wine bottles in the recycle bin and put the glasses in the sink.

Sky didn't understand how her alcohol-soaked mind could still function. *Thank God I'm not on call this weekend.* She swayed from side to side praying she didn't fall over.  On her way to her bedroom, Sky had to focus hard.  She placed one barefoot in front of the other while holding onto the wall.

Tomorrow's headache was going to be a bitch.  *Men*.  This is what they did to women.  Causing them to act out of character and Steven wasn't even her man, yet there she was drunk as a skunk.  Sky couldn't imagine how she would react if she ever truly gave her heart away and it was being toyed with.  Well, she could, and it would probably make an episode of *Snapped*.

In an effort to be more compassionate, Sky continued to ponder how she would have reacted to Nia's situation if she had been in her shoes.  *I would never be in that situation because I wouldn't allow anyone to exert that much power and certainly not a man.  They just weren't worth it.*

Miraculously, Sky made it to her bedroom without falling over herself.  She didn't bother taking off her clothes as she face-planted into the center of her bed and fell into a deep sleep.

# Chapter 2

Remington Kneeland was in a meeting when he received a phone call that no parent ever wanted to receive. "Wait. *What*? Say that again. Bella, I can't understand you." His ex-wife's words were garbled as they tumbled over themselves.

Without saying anything to the men at the table, Remington got up and left the conference room. He thought Bella said that Charlie was hurt.

"This isn't my fault!" She screamed hysterically into the phone.

"What's not your fault? I can barely understand you." Remington covered his ear and plugged it with one finger hoping it would help him hear more clearly. "Calm down and tell me what happened."

"She fell off of her *h-h*-horse and was hurt. She was unconscious when they brought her to the hospital. She is being examined now. She was so pale, Remi."

His heart stopped. Forming coherent thoughts was difficult. "It's almost three a.m. there?" He yelled into the phone. "What the hell was she doing out this late and on a horse in the first place?" Remington took a deep breath to calm down. "How bad is she?"

Bella hesitated. "They don't know if she's going to . . . *make it.* They have to remove part of her skull to release the pressure on her brain. She has some internal injuries and might have to have an operation on her spine, depending on what the tests show."

His knees buckled. Fortunately, he was standing next to a wall. It kept him upright. Remington squeezed his eyes shut and pinched the bridge of his nose. "Who's performing the surgery?"

"Dr. Noah Bridges. And if the spinal cord surgery is necessary, they said one of the best on staff."

"That means nothing if the facility is a chicken shack! I want the best in the country!"

"We don't have time to fly anyone in!"

"What the fuck, Bella? Head trauma? Possible spinal cord injury? How did this happen?!"

"We can discuss that when you get here. In the meantime, they need you to sign some papers and send them back. I had them emailed over to your assistant."

Remington was numb. "What's the name of the surgeon?"

"Dr. Noah Bridges. He's also the Assistant-Chief-of-Staff and is with her now. I'll have him call you, and, if necessary, Dr. Sky Kirby. She is the specialist for the spinal cord injury. She is on her way to the hospital just in case. I'll know more once she arrives."

Ashleigh, Remington's assistant, had stepped out of the conference room moments before just as she was mentioned. Remington motioned for her while talking to Bella. "Have Dr. Bridges call me on this number. I'm on my way." After he hung up, Remington turned to his PA. "Give my excuses. Use my electronic signature to sign whatever papers Bella had sent over and have them bring the car around. Find out who Dr. Sky Kirby is and get her on the phone. As a matter of fact, get her a police escort to St. Lucia's Hospital. I need the plane ready to go within the hour."

Furiously, Ashleigh took notes. "Of course, Mr. Kneeland." Her eyebrows furrowed with worry. "Is everything okay?"

"No. Not at all."

# Chapter 3

Sky was asleep and buried so deep underneath the covers it would take a group like the US Special Forces to find her—*or the hospital*. They seem to always be able to locate her.

Her cell phone vibrated on the nightstand next to her bed.

Given the nature of her job, Sky never slept too soundly. After the second buzz, she reached up into the darkness to answer it. Her voice was muffled since she barely raised her head off the pillow to speak. "Dr. Kirby."

"Sky. It's me."

Inwardly, she groaned. "Noah, I have to be at the hospital in a few hours. I'm not in the mood for company."

"Way to let me know you miss me after your man-bashing weekend with Nia. Anyway, this isn't a social call. I have a twelve-year-old girl with a spinal cord injury. The lumbar vertebrae was badly damaged. It's a mess in there."

Immediately, Sky sat up and flipped on the lamp. "Are you keeping it cold? It's important to make sure those nerves remain viable."

"They're following protocol."

"Good." Sky hopped out of bed. "I'm getting dressed now. I should be there within half-an-hour."

"Look, I'm just going to be honest, I'm not sure there's anything that can be done to fix her but figured you'd want to take a look.  I should warn you the patient is actress Bella Lord-Langston's daughter."

The lightbulb went off in Sky's head.  *"Ahh . . .* you called me because the press is going to be all over this as soon as the sun comes up." He was taking extra precautions, covering himself if things didn't go well.

"They will.  I'll need you to make sure you're *on.*  Considering."

Sky had handled several high-profile patients in the past, and while Noah was a good surgeon, as well as the Assistant-Chief-of-Staff, he had never achieved the level of surgical success that she had.  He was, however, a great politician thus his position.  Given that, she thought it was interesting he was giving *her* medical advice.  "Considering what?"

"Let's just say I hope all the wine you consumed on Friday is out of your system."

"Are you serious?  I would never touch a patient if I were incapacitated in any way."

"Just want to make sure."

After her binge session with Nia, she had spent the past two days in bed recovering.  Sky was fine.  It also helped to have a father who drank entirely too much, and because he did, had a recipe for every type of hangover.  She'd spoken to him the morning after.

"Is your name, Dr. Franklin Johnston?"

"No. I know exactly who I am. My name is Dr. Noah *the shit* Bridges. It should be a name that makes you tingle all over. The ladies love my dark hair that falls just a little bit into my sexy deep blue eyes. Some women have even mistaken me for Ian Somerhalder." He said it with a haughty arrogance.

"Well, Dr. Bridges, right now, I'm not tingling. And you are not my father or Ian. My dad is the only man who can question me. Even *he* knows where to draw the line. *You* need to remember that. I've got to go. See you in twenty." Pissed, Sky disconnected the call.

She made a quick trip to the bathroom before getting dressed. Just as she was zipping up her grey hoodie and about to stick her feet into a pair of sliders, her phone buzzed again. Sky grabbed it off the table as she was leaving the room. She didn't even try to hide her frustration. "I'm walking out of my condo now."

"Good. I have a squad car waiting outside your building to escort you."

It was a deep voice with a sexy timbre she didn't recognize. *That* voice made her tingle. "Excuse me. Who is this?"

"This is Remington Kneeland. I'm calling because you are one of the physicians treating my daughter. I was hoping you could update me on her condition and provide some assurances about her care. The bottom line is, I need to know if you can handle the challenge of saving Charlie's life."

Sky hoisted her back-pack over her shoulder as she stepped onto the elevator. "I'm not God, but in an O.R., I'm pretty damned close. If it can be done, I can do it. Sometimes, if it *can't* be done, I can do it. However, I

16

haven't examined her yet. Therefore, I can't update you about her condition. Until I know what I'm dealing with, you're going to have to depend on the Man above for your assurances."

"Call me as soon as you've examined her." Remington didn't ask but demanded. "I'm currently on my way back from China. I should be there sometime tomorrow evening. You should know that I've contacted Dr. Thomas Henson. He's the top surgeon in this field, and he should be arriving shortly after me. No offense, but I need the best."

Sky's ego took a sucker punch to the gut. She stepped out of the elevator and walked outside her building through the revolving doors. The valet had already brought her Mercedes around the circular drive. Parked directly behind it was the police car. Once the officer noticed her, he turned on his flashing lights.

Sky wasn't impressed. All people should be treated equally. The differences between the haves and have-nots were just too vast to ignore. She was sure her voice came off icier than intended. "Dr. Henson has an impeccable reputation. I've met him once or twice." While Sky had tremendous respect for him, she simply thought she was a much better surgeon—even if she wasn't a household name—*yet*. "If it were my daughter I would want the best for her too." She slid into the driver's seat. Since they were putting all of their cards on the table, Sky let it rip. "I understand that this must be a tough time for you, and I'm sorry. Unless I give you permission to contact me on my private number, call me on the hospital line."

Irritated, she ended the call and stepped on the gas en route to St. Lucia's Hospital.

# Chapter 4

Noah pulled up a chair in one of the private waiting rooms for high-profile patients and sat across from Bella and Kane Langston. The striking pair seemed eager for answers. Kane's arm was draped around his wife's petite frame. He held her close in an attempt to offer comfort. Their look of terror had intensified the moment he walked into the room and with good reason. The news was grim at best, better than the worst-case scenario—but not by much.

Noah didn't mince words. "As I told you when Charlie was brought in to the emergency room, her injuries are severe. We were able to relieve some of the pressure on her brain, but as suspected, she's sustained some internal bleeding and is going to need surgery on her spine. The surgeon I mentioned earlier, Dr. Sky Kirby should be here soon."

Bella clutched her blouse at the center of her chest and crushed it between her fingers. She was afraid to ask her next question. "Will Charlie be okay?" She was barely able to get the words out.

"We are doing everything we can." Noah attempted to remain sensitive as he explained the situation. "Charlie's head trauma is serious, and her spine has been severely damaged."

"Oh, Gaawd." Bella turned her face into her husband's chest.

Noah directed his next words to Kane. "Dr. Kirby is one the best surgeons we have on staff, and I will be assisting."

"That's not good enough." Bella lashed out. "We need the best!"

"I can assure you. It doesn't get much better than Ms. Kirby. I'm not going to sugar coat this. If Charlie makes it through the surgery, *and the night*, it is possible your daughter may never be able to use her extremities."

Bella gasped.

Noah continued. "We won't be able to ascertain any brain damage until after the swelling goes down."

"You mean if there is damage it could be permanent?"

"Yes. Because we won't know the extent of her injuries, we won't have an understanding of what that will mean for Charlie's quality of life." *If she lives, she could be a vegetable,* he thought.

Bella's cries got louder. She suddenly couldn't breathe as her body shook with fear. She couldn't imagine Charlie dying, never walking again, or . . . *what Remington was going to do when he found out what had happened to her*. All the scenarios playing out in her mind were impossible to process. Bella turned her tear-streaked face up toward Kane. "If Charlie pulls through, Remington is going to use this against me for custody."

"*Shh.* Don't think about that. I'll handle Remington." Kane rubbed has palm up and down his wife's back as he rocked Bella in his arms.

She wasn't reassured by Kane's words. Nobody really *handled* Remington. His love for Charlie was the only tool she had to keep him somewhat under control.

Dr. Bridges was irritated that they were discussing a possible custody battle when the girl was fighting for her life. His voice reflected it when he stood. He was gruff. "Has anyone talked to Mr. Kneeland? We need to get the necessary paperwork completed *ASAP*."

Bella would have rather detached her fingernails from her nail bed than call her ex-husband, but she hadn't had a choice. "I called and told him that you would follow-up." Bella reached into her designer purse and handed Dr. Bridges a business card with Remington's information on it.

Noah took it. "Good. The sooner, the better."

# Chapter 5

Noah finished his phone call with Remington Kneeland. He needed to take a quick detour to his office, which was on the fifth floor. The man was too arrogant for words. He was used to snapping his fingers and having people jump. This was a situation *The Great Rich One* couldn't control, and it was eating him alive. *Good,* Noah thought. It was unfortunate that Remington's karma came at the expense of his daughter, but nobody could control karma. Men like him needed to be humbled.

It didn't matter that some people would say that Noah was the same type of man as Remington only with considerably less zeros in his bank account.

Noah stepped inside his office and turned on the lights. He wasn't the least bit surprised to see his latest temptation. She was sitting provocatively on the edge of his desk in her nursing uniform. She was every man's fantasy. Her timing was terrible, but the woman was an enticement too hard to ignore. "What are you doing here?"

Jazlyn purred as she moved her dark hair out of her face and curled her body into his. "I heard about your latest emergency and thought I would help you take the edge off. How long do we have until she arrives?"

Noah agreed that he could certainly use a little edge control as he glanced at his watch. It would be cutting it close, but . . . "Enough." He pulled Jazlyn's mouth to his and kissed her hard on the lips.

She pulled back slightly and stared into his crystal blue eyes. "Wait, before I forget, I wanted to ask if I can assist in the Kneeland surgery." She whispered into his lips. "It could make my career."

Noah knew this was the real reason Jazlyn was in his office. *Not. Going. To. Happen.* "This isn't a good time. You know how Sky is. She likes things done a certain way. I told you to be patient. Everything will happen in due time."

Jazlyn was undeterred. She dragged the tips of her nails up and down his arm. "You've been saying that for months. Now is as good a time as any to push the envelope. Her regular surgical nurse is out of town. She'll need someone tonight, and you could put in a good word for me." Jazlyn placed a wet kiss on that sensitive spot behind his ear. Her tongue darted out and caressed it. "You do me this one little favor, and I promise to do *anything* you want."

Jazlyn was tempting as Noah's eyes focused on the open buttons of her uniform that exposed creamy, full breasts. Who didn't want a hot nurse? He sure as hell did, but her demands were insane. There was no way Noah would allow Sky to be in the same room with Jazlyn, let alone the confined space of an O.R. Sky was the kind of woman a man married. She had a promising future and was good for his career. Jazlyn, on the other hand, was a dime a dozen and would do anything to get ahead. She would have no problem telling Sky everything about their affair if she thought it would advance her career.

Noah had to put an end to what they were doing. But for now, he covered her lips with his and promised himself that he would end things *after* one last quickie. "We'll see."

Something resembling a commitment appeared to be enough for Jazlyn.

All thoughts of surgery were pushed into the recesses of their minds as they engaged in a frenzy of frantic movements. Hands and arms were everywhere as they melted into each other. Soft moans escaped them as their tongues waged war with one another.

They were so caught up in each other that they had no idea how their lives were about to change.

*****

Sky took the elevator up to the fifth floor. When she got off, she headed directly to the O.R. wing. She swiped her badge across the security scanner and pushed through the big double doors as she made her way down the long hallway to the nurse's station.

"Oh, shit!" Cassie saw her on the monitor. She leaned over and whispered into Liam's ear. "Is that Dr. Sky Kirby?"

He looked up from a chart he had been reviewing to study the small screen. "Yep. That is her. Damn that woman is fine in anything, even those gray sweats and hoodie. Hard to believe she's a doctor."

Cassie smacked him in his chest. "Women can be both beautiful *and* smart, you know."

Liam whistled under his breath as Sky approached. "*Mmmhmm.* She is living proof of that." His mouth watered as he watched Sky move toward them. "Even her walk is sexy." She could easily star in any of his fantasies. Even in sweats, Liam could make out her slim waist and rounded hips. He had seen her from behind before and knew Sky had an apple bottom. It took a Herculean effort not to stare her down like a tasty snack when she arrived at the desk. However, Liam prevailed. Both he and Cassie stood a little straighter. He cleared his throat and kept his voice professional. It was also a couple of octaves lower than normal. "Good morning, Dr. Kirby."

Cassie's head turned slightly to glance up at him, but she kept her facial expression serious, even though she wanted to burst out laughing. Still, she couldn't help herself. "Liam? I didn't know you had a cold?"

He ignored her.

Sky was focused and hadn't really seen or heard them. It wasn't every day she was given an opportunity to exercise her surgical talents to this extent. She typically performed one or two procedures daily but based on the images sent to her phone, not one as complicated as what lie ahead. Her heart pounded with anticipation. There were butterflies in her stomach, not from fear but from excitement. It wasn't that Sky was happy someone was hurt; it was quite the opposite. She was crackling with energy to test her skills and do the impossible. Sky was sure she felt like any rock star right before a big performance.

A handsome young man cleared his throat, and the two people standing in front of her came into focus. Sky came down from her cloud just low enough to ask a question. "Is there a chart for Charlie Kneeland?"

This time Cassie answered. "Yes, Dr. Kirby. I have it right here." Quickly, she grabbed the chart and handed it over.

"Thank you." Sky scanned it. Without looking up, she asked another question. "Do you know where I can find Dr. Bridges?"

"I saw him earlier. He was headed toward the physicians' offices." Cassie smiled as she continued to hold her excitement within the walls of her chest.

Sky nodded. "Thanks." She finally looked up and glanced at young woman's nametag. "Cassie."

As Sky walked away and out of earshot, the young nurse behaved as if she had just seen Beyoncé. She hopped up and down, grabbed hold of Liam's arm, and whisper-yelled, "She said my name. She said, Cassie!"

She craned her neck around to the right and left, looking for her partner in crime. "Where is Jazlyn? She will never believe it."

Liam hunched his shoulders. "Not sure. I think she said she needed to use the bathroom about fifteen minutes ago." He pretended to ignore his overly giddy coworker and picked up the paperwork he'd been studying before the appearance of Dr. Kirby. He teased. "I didn't know doctors had groupies."

Cassie laughed. "You're just jealous she didn't notice your sexy charms, especially when you transformed into Barry White." She mimicked him. "*Good morning, Dr. Kirby.*" They both stared at each other before bursting out into hushed laughter.

*****

Sky walked quickly to the physicians' offices, hoping to find Noah. He said he would be down by the emergency but wasn't there. Her soft gym shoes didn't make a sound as she padded down the long hallway. It seemed even longer because of the mostly empty spaces due to the time of night, or morning, depending on how one looked at it.

Sky was still looking over the Kneeland chart when she arrived at Noah's office. The door was closed. A sliver of light was shining underneath it and through the frosted window pane next to the door.

Slowly, she turned the knob and pushed. She stopped short.

*Well, I wasn't expecting this.* Sky stood at the threshold of the door, not really shocked but maybe a little thrown off balance.

*Didn't men have an off switch? Apparently, not.*

There was Noah in vivid Technicolor with some nurse locked in a heated embrace. Sky leaned against the wall and crossed her legs at the ankle, taking in the show. They were so into each other that they hadn't even noticed she was standing in the room. After a moment, or two, she checked her watch, then pulled out her cell phone and snapped a picture before announcing her presence. "If this isn't a good time, I can come back?"

# Chapter 6

Noah immediately released his hold on Jazlyn and jumped away from her as if she had burned him. He stuttered while adjusting his clothes and re-zipping his pants. "S-Sky . . . this isn't w-what it looks like."

Jazlyn shook her head up and down in agreement as her eyes darted from Noah to Sky. She was smart enough not to utter a word.

Sky folded her arms across her chest. "Funny, it looked like you two were throat fucking to me."

Noah turned to Jazlyn. "You should go."

"Yes, Dr. Bridges." She scampered out as fast as she could giving Sky a wide birth as she walked around her.

Sky kept her eyes trained on Noah and wouldn't even spare the woman a glance. However, Sky chuckled as she mimicked her words. *"Dr. Bridges.* My, aren't we suddenly so formal."

Noah thought Sky would be angry. She seemed more annoyed than anything. She should be screaming and yelling. Instead, she stood in total control, seemingly mocking them. He didn't understand it and prayed this wasn't the calm before the storm. He needed to figure out what was going on inside her head. That's when he began to explain. "Look, Jazlyn means nothing to me."

"I stopped caring about how you felt and what you thought about five seconds ago." Sky pushed herself off the wall and walked toward him. "Did we get all the release forms signed to perform the surgery?"

He hesitated before speaking. "Yes. I spoke to Remington Kneeland. His office sent over the necessary paperwork."

"Good. Then, if that's settled, I need a nursing assistant. Since you've worked with both Cassandra Meadows and Jazlyn Farrow, who's the best? I'm sorry. Let me rephrase that. Who's the better nurse? Just so we're clear, I'm looking for surgical experience, not the kind where you include rutting like animals."

He sighed. "Sky . . ."

She cut him off. "Look, nothing else matters right now except for finding someone qualified to assist me. You may be a lousy human, but you're a good surgeon and have worked with both of the women."

Frustrated, Noah swiped his hand through his thick, dark hair. "Are you serious? You don't want to talk about what just happened? I can't believe you'd even consider Jazlyn as an option to help you."

"Again, you take me for someone who actually gives a shit about either of you. The patient deserves the best. If she can help me put that little girl back together again, then that's all that matters. After that, I don't ever have to deal with either of you again."

"That's impossible. We work together. I made a mistake. Don't let one mistake ruin us."

"*You* ruined us, and *you* decided there was no *us* the moment you started sleeping with someone else. You could have at least told me we weren't exclusive so that I could have had other options too." Sky looked down at her chart. "Both of their records are equally impressive."

Frustrated, Noah began to pace. "Are you a robot or something?! We've been dating for months, and you're acting like I didn't mean *anything* to you!"

Sky hissed. "No, that would be you!" She pointed the metal chart at him. "Not me. So, stop confusing me with some twenty-two-year-old brain dead *idiot*, and quit trying to run your psycho-babble-bullshit game on me."

"That's not what I'm trying to do. I messed up. I'm sorry. I had a momentary lapse in judgment. You mean so much to me."

He reached for Sky, but she backed away and glared at him. "If I were important, I would have never walked in on you playing tonsil hockey and about to do God only knows what else with that woman."

"Are you that cold?"

"Cold? That's rich." Those words had been thrown at her before, but she refused to let them hurt her. *REFUSED* to allow him to hit her where she was vulnerable. She wasn't cold or unfeeling, at least, not with the people who earned her trust. Even before tonight, Noah hadn't earned it. But after tonight, he'd failed just like all of the rest. "Look, we don't have time for this. If you can't tell me which one of the nurses is the best, I'll flip a coin."

He lashed out. "Maybe if you had shown me that you cared even a little." He placed his thumb and forefinger together. "This incident would never have occurred." His face was red with frustration. Nothing he said seemed to be breaking through.

*This bastard is still trying to blame this on me?* Sky was about to cut-up then stopped herself. She wasn't going to allow him to pull her into his circle of madness.

"Wow. *Dr. Bridges,* your ego has caused you to lose your mind as well as overestimate your importance to me. I'll be scrubbed and ready for surgery in ten minutes. I hope you can get yourself together in that amount of time. You seem a little *emotional*, and Charlie Kneeland needs you at the top of your game." Sky started to walk away.

Noah knew that Sky had intimacy issues, and this situation wouldn't help that. She had emotionally walled him off and was not going to allow him back into her space, at least, not yet. He'd messed up. Smooth words and charm were not going to fix things. He saw it in her eyes. Reluctantly, he answered the question. "Meadows."

Sky stopped walking, and without turning around, she responded. "Meadows it is." She refused to give him, or anyone else for that matter, the satisfaction of knowing they could hurt her. Fortunately, the O.R. was a place she could focus on what really mattered, and that was saving lives and not on her latest disappointment. It was her place of Zen and probably saved her thousands in therapy costs.

Sky left his office and quickly went over toward the nurse's station where she came face-to-face with Jazlyn again. The woman shrank back from her gaze as if attempting to disappear. There was no need for that, but Sky understood why she would. Jazlyn Farrow had to know that Sky could end her career with the snap of a finger. Even though Sky could, she wouldn't. Decisions based on emotions never worked out in the end. And no man was worth throwing an entire career away. She hated women who thought they could climb the ladder of success by lying on their backs. If Jazlyn continued on the path she was on, she would end her own career.

Sky stopped and turned her attention toward the other woman. "Cassie, right?"

"Yes, Dr. Kirby?" She couldn't believe the woman remembered her name.

"Can you be scrubbed up and ready for surgery in the next ten minutes?"

Cassie was about to levitate off the ground. "Absolutely. I can be ready in five."

"Good. I hope you've eaten your Wheaties because this procedure is going to be a marathon."

"I have my running shoes ready and have been preparing my whole life for this."

That was the kind of enthusiasm Sky liked to hear. She lifted a perfectly sculpted eyebrow. "If you can be ready in five, then I'll see you in three." Seeing the excitement on Cassie's face helped to distract from Noah's lying and cheating, Sky thought as she walked away.

It wasn't until she was alone in the physicians' locker room and changing into her scrubs that Sky allowed herself a moment to take a deep breath. She had hoped Noah would be different. On paper, he was perfect, and she had thought maybe he could be the one. Instead, he had lived up to her low expectations of men.

She tucked her mass of dark, wiry curls underneath her surgical cap. *How many times am I going to do this dance?* She was good and truly over liars and broken promises. In the past, Sky contemplated getting a dog. Maybe she needed to do more than just think about it. A dog might be the closest she would ever come to a healthy relationship. While she wasn't an advocate of making emotional decisions, Sky was going to make an exception. "Time to get a pooch." At least they had a reputation for being loyal.

Her phone vibrated in her pocket. She took it out and answered it. "Dr. Kirby."

"Any updates on my daughter?"

Sky looked around the room as if the man were hiding behind the lockers. "I thought I told you not to call me at this number?"

"Two things. One, I don't take orders very well. Two, why wouldn't I call this number? It's the best way to reach you."

"Mr. Kneeland, I am on my way into surgery *now*. You of all people should want me calm. Harassing me right before I put a scalpel in my hand is not a good way to accomplish that."

He sighed heavily into the phone. "I hate feeling helpless."

Sky massaged her forehead. The despair in his voice touched her. "Look, how about you make yourself useful and Google me. I may not be a household name like Dr. Henson, but my credentials are pretty damned impressive if I say so myself. I am hanging up now. I have a really important patient waiting for me." Sky pressed the end button and turned off her phone. She placed it in her locker and shut the door.

"It's go time."

# Chapter 7

After sixteen hours, Charlie Kneeland's surgery was over.  Sky and Noah walked out of the operating room physically exhausted.  The most challenging part of their work, though, still lay ahead.

Sky pulled off her surgical cap as they approached the room where Bella and Kane were waiting for updates about the procedure.

"Dr. Kirby?"  Cassie called out to Sky as she exited the O.R.

"Yes?"  Sky wasn't able to keep the exhaustion out of her voice when she responded.

"I just wanted to thank you for allowing me to assist.  It was a great educational experience, and I learned so much.  Is it okay if I make a few copies of the things I want to review from the surgery and get a copy of your final report to compare to my own notes?"

Sky was impressed with Cassie's work ethic.  "Of course.  I'll have someone email it to you. Make sure you study up, so next time, you'll know what I need before I ask."

*Next time*.  Cassie was on cloud nine and beamed.  "Absolutely!  Thank you again for the opportunity."  She backed away and headed toward the locker room.

"I guess she didn't think much of my skills."  Noah laughed but deep down it bothered him.  He had been rendered invisible during Sky's exchange with Cassie.  It happened a lot when they worked together.  He played off his jealousy with a smile that didn't reach his blue eyes.  "You were brilliant today." Noah reached out to touch Sky's hand, but she snatched it away. He stared into her big beautiful brown eyes, pleading with her to forgive him in the hopes that they could share this experience together. Maybe it could serve as a reset for their relationship.

Sky glanced away. It would be so easy to confuse the energy derived from performing what she hoped was a successful surgery and misdirect it to something, or *someone,* else. Sky refused to allow that to happen. Slowly, she exhaled. "Let's just get this over with."

Disappointed, Noah forged ahead. He used the back of his knuckles to tap on the door. When there was no response, he knocked again a little harder before pushing the door open and slowly walking inside.

Bella and Kane were fully clothed, lying across a bed sleeping. Noah coughed in an attempt to wake them. "Excuse me. Mr. and Mrs. Langston?"

Sky had no idea how they could even nod off at a time like this.

Bella's head snapped up. Anxiously, she roused her husband awake. They sat up and got out of bed. Bella's voice shook slightly. "How is my daughter?"

Sky knew the woman was terrified, but what she didn't know was the source of it. Was it the fear that Charlie might die or that she might live to tell a few secrets? Sky shook her head to chase away those thoughts.

Noah was relieved to be able to give her the news. "Charlie is a fighter. She is tough. The surgery went well."

Sky folded her arms across her chest and remained silent as she watched their reaction to the news.

"Will she be alright?" Nervously, Bella rubbed her hands together.

Noah responded. "We won't know for a little while yet. There is quite a bit of swelling. Once it goes down, we'll know if the nerves have fused together properly and are talking to each other."

Kane squeezed his wife's hand when he asked, "Is she going to live?"

His concern seemed forced. Sky narrowed her eyes. "I hope so because I'd like to ask her how she got those bruises all over her body. They certainly didn't come from tonight's *accident*." Sky leveled suspicious eyes toward Bella and Kane. "Any ideas on how it could have happened?"

"Bruises?" Bella stuttered. "I-I don't know what you're talking about—"

Kane cut in. "We don't know anything about any bruising. Charlie was fine before tonight. If there were some unusual marks on her body, more than likely, it came from this hospital."

The tension in the air was thick. Noah attempted to bring it down. "Charlie's body has gone through a lot. The next twenty-four hours are going to be critical. Fortunately, she is healthy. That will work in her favor." Noah glanced at Sky, chastising her with his eyes and demanding she stand down. "Dr. Kirby and I will be hanging around for a while. If you have any questions, don't hesitate to contact *me*." He stressed the *me* instead of *us*. "In the meantime, you and Mrs. Langston do your best to get some rest. It's going to be a long night." He shook both their hands.

38

Sky did not. Instead, she leveled a hard stare at Noah, Kane, and Bella before walking out of the room.

Once they were out of earshot, Noah turned to Sky. "What the hell was that?"

"Something is not right, and you know it. That girl had bruises everywhere. How do we know that she fell off of a horse? What in God's name would she have been doing on one at that time of morning? It doesn't make sense."

"You don't know her or her family. That could be the time they go horseback riding! This is unlike you to jump to unfounded conclusions! Don't let our issues cloud your judgment. Charlie's injuries are consistent with falling off a horse, and if her parents say that's what happened, then that's what happened."

Sky hissed. "Your ego is out of control. Charlie's injuries are also consistent with abuse."

"You're going too far. I just told you—we can't make assumptions like that if we don't have any facts to back them up."

"We don't?" Sky was angry that he wasn't connecting the dots. "Noah, those bruises were at least a couple of days old. Kane and Bella are both acting suspiciously. We have an obligation to our patient to contact children and family services. As attending physician, you should have done that the moment you examined her in the emergency room! They can investigate, and if they don't find anything, we will have done what we were supposed to do."

He grabbed her hard by the arm. "Are you crazy?  That's Bella Lord!  Her PR team would be all over us."

Sky snatched her arm out of his grip.  "I don't care who she is!  I'm not turning a blind eye."

"You can't unilaterally call anyone.  There is a protocol for high-profile clients.  You've got to discuss this with the Chief-of-Staff.  He won't approve it, and as the Assistant Chief-of-Staff, I won't back you up.  I'm not losing my career or reputation as a physician over your unfounded suspicions."

"You spineless weasel!  I can't believe I ever thought . . ." Sky let her words fade.

"Call me whatever names you want.  I'm not committing career suicide on a little girl who might not live through the next twenty-four hours."

"You're disgusting."  Horrified, Sky backed away from him shaking her head.

*****

Two hours later, Sky had taken a shower and a nap in her office.  She typically didn't leave the hospital for the first twenty-four hours after a procedure as complex as the one she had just performed.  When she woke up, she checked on Charlie and then her other patients before coming back to her corner of the world to eat the Chinese food she had ordered.

Sky sat at her desk with her chin resting on one hand and eating shrimp fried rice out of the box with a set of chopsticks. She had been surfing the internet looking for a rescue dog when her cell phone rang. She put down her food and sticks to answer it. "Hey, Nia."

"Hey, you. How did the surgery go?"

"I won't know for a little while."

"I'm sure you did the best you could."

"I did. I just hope it was enough." She thought about mentioning her suspicions regarding Charlie to Nia but then changed her mind.

"Must be nice working side by side with Noah like that."

"Not when you want to punch him in the face."

"Whoa . . . for what? What did he do?"

"I got a not-so-surprising surprise."

"Uh-oh. What?"

"Let's just say stick a fork in us. We're done."

"Are you serious?" Nia wasn't all that surprised, despite him lasting longer than most.

"Yep."

Nia sighed. "Did he leave his shoes in the hallway instead of by the door?"

"Ha, ha. Very funny." Sky held the phone between her ear and shoulder as she picked up the box of rice and started eating again. "Actually, I interrupted him about to have sex with another woman."

Nia went silent before yelling into the phone. "Oh. My. Gaawd! I'm so sorry. What a pig! What did he say for himself?"

"What could he say? *I. Saw. Him*! I literally caught him minutes before we were supposed to go into surgery."

"Did you beat her ass?"

Sky's hand froze with the chop-sticks half-way to her mouth. "Why would I do that?"

"Because she was about to *get it in* with your man!"

"Did you beat up the woman who cheated with Steven?"

"I would have if I could have caught her. She ran out of the apartment too fast. I mean she literally left butt naked." Nia laughed.

Sky didn't see the humor, especially when it had only happened a couple of nights ago. She shook her head in disgust. Nia had obviously taken that slimeball back. She didn't have to say it. Nia's jovial mood told the tale.

"Anyway, weren't you all about doing memorable and lasting damage?" Nia reminded her.

Though Nia couldn't see Sky, she shrugged her shoulders. "True. But the difference in our situations was that you actually loved Steven. You two had years of shared history together. I just kind of liked Noah. We were only dating for few months. I wasn't that emotionally attached. I was angrier with myself for not trusting my instincts than with him." Sky changed the subject. She didn't want to give Noah any more of her time. "I'm guessing your therapy session with Steven went well?"

Nia wasn't so sure that Sky wasn't hurt. It was genuinely hard to tell since she hid her feelings so well. "We are still trying to find a time that works with both of our schedules."

"Mmmhmm." Sky took another bite of her food.

"I won't let you deflect. Noah's betrayal has got to make you feel some kind of way."

"It does. Angry. Seriously, I was uncomfortable for all of five minutes. Noah did exactly what I expected. I dodged a bullet. He's a narcissistic social-climbing ball of phlegm. I don't need him in my life."

"That's um . . . disgusting. You work with the man. How do you plan to avoid him?"

"I'm a professional. I can separate my work from my personal life."

Nia's voice softened. "Did he apologize?"

"Doesn't matter."

"Yes, it does. We all make mistakes."

Sky wasn't settling for the bullshit like Nia. "I don't. If I give you my word or make a commitment, I keep it. I also don't put my career ahead of doing what's right."

"Well, that sounds . . . *cryptic*. Even so, we all can't be as perfect as you."

"I'm not perfect, just consistent."

"That was sarcasm. No, you are not perfect. That's my point."

"Dr. Kirby?" A deep male voice boomed through Sky's office, interrupting her and Nia's conversation.

Sky almost dropped her phone. It took her by surprise because it was late, and she wasn't expecting anyone. She bobbled the cell in her hand before getting control of it. Her eyes locked on to the face of an incredibly handsome man standing in her office doorway. Her mouth went dry, and her insides clenched. Sky had never had this visceral of a reaction to a man before in her life. It didn't matter that his suit was wrinkled, and his face had day old growth on it.

He repeated her name. "Dr. Sky Kirby?" His voice was familiar, and then she remembered—*Remington Kneeland.*

Sky scrambled to make sure her face was blank as she swallowed. Then she remembered Nia was on the phone. Sky wasn't sure how much, if anything, he may have heard of their conversation but refused to give anything away by her expression. Sky whispered into the receiver. "Nia, I'll have to call you back." She disconnected the line, slid the phone back into her pocket, and stood.

"Yes, I'm Dr. Kirby." She extended her hand.

The man shook it. "I'm Remington Kneeland, Charlie's father. They told me I should find you before going to the I.C.U." Worry lines were etched all over his face. "I came straight from the airport. How is she?"

Talking to him in person was much different than over the phone. The anguish on his face made her feel the compassion she hadn't felt enough of earlier. "Please have a seat."

"I'd rather stand, thank you." His voice was gruff. Even though his body language screamed exhaustion, Remington straightened his six-foot-three-inch frame as if bracing for the worst.

Sky nodded. "Charlie is holding her own. She's in critical but stable condition. Dr. Bridges performed a craniectomy and assisted me in the spinal cord by-pass procedure."

"Can you explain that to me in layman's terms?"

"I'm sorry. A craniectomy had to be performed to relieve the pressure on Charlie's brain. That is where a small portion of the skull is removed due to severe swelling. A separate procedure was necessary to repair some damaged nerves. We attempted to fuse them back together. Unfortunately, some of them were damaged beyond repair. However, I was able to take intact peripheral nerves rostral to the level of injury and transfer them into the spinal cord below the injury. I tried to call you once the procedure was finished but your phone went to voicemail."

"We must have been flying over a blind spot, and I haven't checked my messages. That all sounds complicated."

"It is very complicated. I don't leave those kinds of messages."

He nodded.  "Not sure I understand all of what you just explained. I'll have to research it."

"Charlie is currently in the I.C.U. and has been placed in a medical coma.  That was necessary to assist in her recovery.  We need her completely still for a while, but it appears that both procedures seemed to go very well."

"Seemed?  When will we know for *sure*?"

"I will be honest with you, Mr. Kneeland.  Charlie's injuries are life-threatening.  The next several hours are going to be critical.  Every hour that she can hang on is crucial.  The longer she remains stable, the better her chances."

Remington couldn't wrap his mind around Sky's words.  How was it possible that one minute Charlie and he were Skyping, and the next, he could lose her?

His anguish was hard to ignore.  It was written all over him, and Sky's heart softened.  It was apparent that Remington was trying to be strong when Sky saw his Adam's apple move up and down as he swallowed.

"What are the chances of a full recovery?"

"I wish I could give you that information.  We just won't have any idea of what we are dealing with until the swelling goes down, and *if*, or when, Charlie regains consciousness.  As of now, we are taking it one step at a time.  With each success, we can focus on any necessary rehabilitation."

Remington was anxious.  "In cases like this, what is considered a normal amount of time to regain consciousness?"

"It really depends on Charlie.  Once we get through these next hours, we will still need to keep her in an induced coma until she reaches certain benchmarks and we're comfortable with her progress.  Then, slowly, we will attempt to bring her out."

Remington had a strong chiseled jawline like the men in the movies. Sky pressed her lips into a firm line because she was feeling a little disgusted with herself for noticing how attractive he was at a time like this.

Remington ran a hand over the unshaven overgrowth on his face as he thought about her words.  "I mentioned to you over the phone that I was calling in a specialist.  Dr. Henson's flight has been delayed.  Provided his flight is on-time, he won't be able to offer a second opinion until tomorrow morning."

His words were like cold water being thrown over her.  "Good to know."  Sky's response was flat.  She knew it was a smart decision to want a second opinion, but it still messed with her ego. *There isn't anyone better than me in this field.*  There were only a few doctors who had ever successfully completed a spinal cord by-pass.  Even Dr. Henson hadn't ever done one successfully.  Sky refrained from saying those words out loud. Instead, she forced a smiled.  "A second opinion is always good.  Do you have any other questions?"

He hadn't really heard what she said until her tone changed.  "I just want Charlie to wake up and be happy and healthy."

"We're doing all we can to make the first part of that happen, Mr. Kneeland."  She almost mentioned her suspicions regarding the bruises on

Charlie but then thought better of it.  Remington had enough on his plate, and Sky didn't have any proof.  She would table it for now, maybe indefinitely.  "If you don't have any other questions, I can take you up to see her."

# Chapter 8

It was late morning, and Sky hadn't left the hospital since the day before. She had been there all night and had slept in her office. She was waiting for Dr. Thomas Henson to arrive, only he hadn't made it into town. His flight schedule kept changing.

After performing back-to-back surgeries, Sky was ready to call it quits and go home for a few hours of rest. Before she could make her escape and dive headlong into her bed, she still needed to finish up her rounds.

Fighting exhaustion, Sky yawned as she arched her lower back and massaged her aching muscles. The moment she walked through the front door of her condo, Sky planned to fall into a deep sleep. *One more patient and it's on.*

*Damn.* She saw him. Dr. Shane Shaw, the hospital's Chief-of-Staff, although he hadn't yet spotted her. His stride was purposeful. Sky cringed on the inside. He was never on patient floors willy-nilly. Hopefully, he was looking for someone else because if he was searching for her, she knew it was about her report. *Pleeeeeeease ask me to consult on a patient and don't ask me about Charlie Kneeland.* She begged the goddesses.

It was too late to turn down a different hallway or get the hell out of dodge. Sky's brain was buzzing, but no escape ideas came to mind. *This would be an excellent time to have a superpower.* If she had one, Sky would make herself disappear.

Seconds later, Dr. Shaw glanced up in her direction.

*Please let him be looking at someone over my shoulder and not at me.* Sky did her best to avoid eye contact. She was acting like a two-year-old, hoping that if she didn't look at him, he wouldn't be able to see her.

"Dr. Kirby?" His booming voice rang out. "I've been looking for you."

*Great. The goddesses weren't answering prayers today.* He didn't look happy either. As a matter of fact, he looked downright angry. Sky took a deep breath and dragged herself toward him. Inwardly, she groaned. *Damn, damn, damn!* On the outside, Sky appeared steely calm. She was sure her demeanor didn't reveal what was really going through her mind. "Dr. Shaw."

"I need a moment of your time."

Sky displayed the practiced art of feigned interest. Just a little scrunch of the forehead added the perfect touch. "Of course." They stood in the middle of the hall next to the nurse's station. Sky placed her hands in her pockets and rocked slightly back and forth on the heels and balls of her feet.

"Our PR department has been working overtime, attempting to keep the Langston-Kneeland situation quiet. I haven't signed off on your report because I'm not sure you were thinking clearly."

At the mention of the Langstons and Kneelands, Sky felt her eyes start to roll into the back of her head but caught herself. Her tone was calm, *even.* "My mind was very clear, and I stand by my assessment. Although I didn't put it in the report, I also feel like we had an obligation to call Child Protective Services the night of the accident, yet did not. As far as the press, they are going to do what they do regardless." She managed to keep the frustration out of her voice.

"It's not our job to give them ammunition."

She nodded. "No, it's not. I certainly would never purposefully do that. However, I hope you are not asking me to make an unethical decision."

"No, but I am challenging your assessment. I spoke with Dr. Bridges, and he seems to have a difference of opinion on the condition of Charlie Kneeland's body when she came into the E.R."

"Of course, he would. He was responsible for making that call, considering his position affords him that luxury of not being forced to adhere to protocol."

"He made a judgment that I agree with completely."

"I saw her bruises." Sky spoke through clenched teeth. "They were not fresh. That girl had been beaten."

Dr. Shaw responded in hushed angry tones. "Trying to determine *what* caused or how old a bruise is based on how it looks is imprecise science at best and you know it."

"They were yellowing. It can take up to eighteen to twenty-four hours after an injury for that color to appear. According to her parents, Charlie Kneeland was brought into the emergency room within an hour of the accident *without* bruises. We should have at least asked questions about them!"

"You know as well as I do that too many variables can affect the creation and resolution of a bruise. The type of tissue injured, mechanism of injury, length, duration of force, depth of injury, skin color, the health status of the patient, medications, and age.  We don't have enough definitive information to go throwing around charges like that.  Remove it from the report.  I won't leave this hospital open for a lawsuit."

*And there it was.*  The priority was to protect the hospital even at the expense of someone's health.  As Dr. Shaw spoke, Sky's mind flashed to the sweet face of the young girl.  She wasn't exactly sure why, but Charlie had managed to garner a healthy dose of empathy from Sky for her.  "Again, you are asking me to change the report, and I cannot do that.  What I wrote is my complete and *final* assessment."

Dr. Shaw was pissed.  "So, you are telling me no?  That could be considered insubordination."

"Call it what you want, but . . ." Sky straightened her spine.  "I am not changing one word."

They glared at each other for what seemed like forever before he spoke again.  "I have another meeting.  We will revisit this later." Dr. Shaw was furious as he stalked away.

Sky was relieved and happy he was gone.  Dr. Shaw knew full well that something other than falling off a horse caused those bruises.  He saw the pictures.  The top brass seemed to be banding together to cover it up. It was disgusting.

Speaking of her famous patient, Sky was on her way to see her. After her run-in with Dr. Shaw, Sky could only hope she wouldn't be bumping heads with Noah anytime soon. At least she knew it wouldn't be today since he wasn't at the hospital.

Sky walked with purpose down the hallway that boasted nothing but white floors and walls and super bright fluorescent lights lining the ceilings. It mirrored how she felt—cold, colorless, lifeless.

As she approached Charlie's room, she heard them before she saw them—Bella and Remington—arguing. They stood outside Charlie's door going at it.

"So, you're leaving?" Remington couldn't believe it.

They were so involved in their discussion that they hadn't even noticed Sky's presence. *Too bad I can't sneak past these crazies.* Her patience was gone. She didn't have any energy left to deal with their issues, and they had plenty of them. She whisper-yelled, "Lower your voices! This is a hospital, not an MMA event. If you can't do that, take your discussion outside and away from my patient."

Bella and Remington turned angry eyes meant for each other at her. Sky didn't care. She could take it. She had had more than enough experience dealing with divorced parents from hell. She only needed to pull from her own personal experiences. Although Bella and Remington had been in the same hospital for less than twenty-four hours, they argued twenty-three of them and stretched Sky past her limits. Sky couldn't imagine how Charlie dealt with it.  She had to have felt like being trapped inside a hurricane.  It wasn't good for her as she fought to recover.

Sky turned her *I mean business glare* first to Bella and then Remington.  Once she was confident they got the message, Sky moved to enter Charlie's room. Bella stopped her by placing a hand over her arm.

"Dr. Kirby, I need to have a word with you.  Since Dr. Bridges is not on call today, you'll have to do."

*No. She. Didn't.*  Sky's eyes narrowed.  "I can always give you Dr. Bridges's *personal* cell phone number?" Noah never answered that phone when he was off, and Sky knew it.  "Especially, since he's better at managing high-maintenance people than I am."

Bella Langston drew back as if she'd been slapped.  She wasn't used to people talking to her in any way other than adoration.  Bella couldn't fire Sky or send her away because she was considered one of the best.  Instead, Bella ignored her snide remark.  When this situation was all over, Bella vowed that Dr. Kirby would be handled.  In the meantime, she took a deep breath and flipped her flowing, golden hair over her shoulders.  "I just wanted to know if you received the paperwork giving Remi complete control over Charlie's medical treatment while I'm out of the country."

Sky nodded.  Her response was clipped.  "I received it, and the hospital staff is aware of the changes." *It was good at least one of Charlie's parents could be bothered with the ordeal of parenting.*  Sky couldn't believe that *the Bella Lord-Langston* was about to abandon her only child less than twenty-four hours after surgery. If nothing else, she would have thought it would be a public relations nightmare. It infuriated her.

Sky refused to give the self-absorbed woman another second of her time, so she pushed forward. "Excuse me. I need to check on your daughter." Sky was surprised she was able to be professional, although her words were laced with anger. She turned the knob and entered the room closing the door behind her.

No one had ever stood up to either Bella or Remington the way Sky had. Instead, of being pissed, Remington was actually *impressed*.

# Chapter 9

World-renowned neurosurgeon, Dr. Thomas Henson exited a black limousine as Dr. Shaw and Noah looked on. Noah was supposed to have the day off but received the call about the visit and came rushing to the hospital specifically for Dr. Henson's consult.

"It is a pleasure to meet you, sir." Noah had stars in his eyes as they shook hands.

Dr. Shane Shaw echoed Noah's sentiments. "It is a great honor to have you in our hospital. Please follow me to my office where we can discuss in more detail the Kneeland case."

They were twenty minutes into the briefing when Dr. Henson asked a question. "Where is the surgeon who performed the spinal cord procedure?"

Shane and Noah looked at each other. "We thought it best that we brief you on the details."

Dr. Thomas Henson crossed his legs and looked at them suspiciously. "Interesting. Thank you for the special attention. However, I want to talk to Dr. Kirby. Unless she is in surgery or out of the country, I expect to see her." He stood. "If you'll excuse me, I need to use the facilities. Do you think you can have her here by the time I return?"

Dr. Henson's question wasn't really a question at all. It was a stern request.

Dr. Shaw nodded. "Of course."

*****

Sky walked into Dr. Shaw's office, and the first face she saw was Remington Kneeland. He was surrounded by her *all* male and white counterparts.

It was clear they had been there for a while. It burned her up inside. How many times did she have to walk into a room and be the only woman and the only *black* person, male or female? It was so frustrating. Despite that fact, she kept it together.

"Dr. Kirby. Glad you could make it." Shane feigned enthusiasm to see her.

She did not return his fake warm welcome. "Turning down a summons by the Chief-of-Staff might be called insubordination. We can't have that on my record can we, gentleman?"

Remington liked her spunk. She had fire in her eyes.

Dr. Henson attempted to hold back a grin. "I've had an opportunity to examine Charlie and review her medical records. I have to say, you performed a procedure less than ten people in the country have attempted successfully, including myself. From what I can tell, it was damn good work. Congratulations, Doctor." He extended his hand to her.

"Thank you, Dr. Henson. It means a lot coming from you. I'm a great admirer of your work." Sky finally brandished a tiny smile and shook his hand. *Respect*. It was all she ever demanded from her peers. He seemed to want to give it without Sky having to demand it.

"I was just informing Remington that I couldn't have done a better job. I'm not even sure I could have done the job you did. I knew there was something special about you when we met at that conference in New York."

"You remember that?"

"Of course. It's not every day you meet a brilliant surgeon."

"Again, thank you, Sir." Sky glanced over at the man whom Dr. Henson had recently referenced. His expression was guarded. He didn't give anything away. He seemed to be taking it all in.

"Well, let's not go that far." Dr. Shaw spoke. "We don't know yet if the procedure will be successful, so we might want to keep the champagne on ice." He seemed to have forgotten, then remembered, that Remington was in the room. "We are very hopeful, Mr. Kneeland."

Sky hadn't realized how much she detested Dr. Shaw until now. She turned accusatory eyes at him. "Maybe someone should tell that to the person who leaked how *groundbreaking* the first *successful* bypass spinal cord surgery performed at St. Lucia's Hospital was."

His face tightened.

Sky relished in his reaction and decided to add more fuel to the fire. "I'm pretty sure that's how they worded it when I saw it in the papers today. Funny how there was no mention of the surgeon who performed it."

Remington's eyes narrowed. Up to this point, he hadn't shown any emotion. He glanced between Dr. Henson and Sky but leveled most of his suspicions at Dr. Shaw. "I really hope for the sake of St. Lucia's that someone from this institution isn't leaking private medical information."

Dr. Shaw moved quickly to reassure him. Though Dr. Henson may have been more well-known, Remington Kneeland was much more powerful. Shaw wanted to stay on his good side. "Of course not. Sky is just being . . . Well, Sky. She gets emotional sometimes. Your privacy is our utmost concern."

"I would hope that my daughter's health is your utmost concern." The edge in Remington's voice could cut through rock.

"Well, yes. Of course. That goes without saying."

Dr. Henson tried to de-escalate the growing tension in the room. "Dr. Kirby?"

She snatched her eyes away from the Chief-of-Staff and back to him. "Yes?"

"Dr. Franklin Johnston is your father? Is that correct?"

"Yes, he is. How did you know?"

"He and I attended medical school together and have kept in touch over the years. Even though you don't use his last name professionally, he has always been very proud of you."

"You are too kind." Professionally, Sky felt the same about her father. Too bad personally, he was a walking disaster.

Dr. Henson clapped his hands together. "I think we've talked enough about the case. I would love to take a tour of the hospital before my flight this afternoon."

Dr. Shaw nodded in agreement. "I think that's a great idea. Since Dr. Bridges will be taking over the entire Kneeland case, it would be a good time to get to know him." He turned to Sky. "If you still have patients to see, please feel free to do that now."

He sucker punched her. Her blood pressure shot through the roof. Did he really think he was going to dismiss her after all the work she'd done and give her patient to Noah? "Wait a minute? What do you mean *I'm off the case*?"

"We can discuss this later, Sky." He said in a dismissive tone.

"That's *Dr. Kirby*! I am a doctor just like the other men in this room. Show me the same goddamn respect! Noah is a great doctor, but he doesn't know a nerve root from the dura. Charlie needs the best care, and I shouldn't be shut out because I don't have a penis swinging between my thighs."

Dr. Shaw's face turned three shades of red. He was not just angry but embarrassed. He lost it. "Have you lost your mind you arrogant, egotistical bit—!?!" He didn't finish what he was going to say. "Don't think for one second that just because you are a gifted surgeon that I won't fire your ass!"

"You won't have to fire me. I quit!" Sky stormed out of the office angrier than she had ever been in her life.

After she left, Dr. Shaw apologized. "I'm sorry, gentleman, that you had to witness some of the ugliness of hospital business. Sky Kirby has always been a difficult woman to deal with."

Remington had had enough. He had spent too much time away from his daughter, dealing with this shit show. He turned steely eyes toward Dr. Shaw. "Difficult or not, Dr. Henson thinks she's the best person to treat my daughter. Therefore, so do I."

"But, Mr. Kneeland—" Dr. Shaw began to protest.

"No buts. Get her back. Fix it." He never raised his voice, but his tone left no room for argument. "Otherwise, wherever Dr. Kirby takes her talents, my money and I will follow." He turned to Dr. Thomas Henson. "Thank you for coming and for your expert opinion." He shook his hand. "If you will excuse me, I think I'm done here." Remington started to walk out of the office. He turned back, looking at Noah. "One more thing, I don't need a physician who doesn't know the difference between whatever the hell it was Dr. Kirby said. I have no need for you or your services."

Noah was furious. He hadn't said or done anything, yet Sky managed to make him look like a sniveling fool in front of some very powerful men.

As he watched Remington's retreating back, Noah vowed that he would make Sky pay for the damage and embarrassment she had caused him.

*****

Sky had boxes on her desk and was packing her things when Remington entered her office. She was also on her phone. "Uh-huh. A

61

misunderstanding. That's what Dr. Shaw is calling it?" She spoke on the phone with Human Resources. "Thank you." Sky disconnected.

"Did he fix it?"

Sky hadn't heard Remington enter her office. She glanced up. The man moved so silently it freaked her out. "Excuse me?" The sound of his voice got to her every time. The man exuded sex appeal.

"I asked if Dr. Shaw gave you your job back."

"Considering I quit, it's interesting you should ask. That was Human Resources on the phone. The woman said that it was all a misunderstanding. I am guessing you had something to do with his sudden change of heart?"

Remington took a seat without being asked. "You might not want to remain at this hospital, but if Doc Henson says you're the best, then Charlie needs you. I hope whatever you do that you keep that in mind."

Sky's decision to leave, or stay, wasn't about the good old boys club. It was about saving lives. She wouldn't allow her justifiable anger to keep her from doing just that. She sighed. "Of course. If you want me to remain Charlie's physician, I will. Sometimes the purpose of things can get a little crazy when egos are involved, and I apologize."

"I apologize too. We got off to a rocky start and haven't really had a chance to talk. When we have, it hasn't been very pleasant." He was tired and dark circles had formed around his eyes. "The bottom line is I can tell you're not only good at what you do but passionate about your work. Charlie's going to need every bit of luck and people like you in her corner."

"Thank you." Sky spoke softly.

Remington got up to leave. "Thank you for what you are doing for Charlie. And let me know if you need anything else. Just say the word, and I'll make it happen."

"All I have to do is just say the word, huh?"

A slow lop-sided grin appeared on Remington's face. "It can't be easy doing what you do even when you're at the top of your game. I just witnessed it first-hand. In this case, your success will hopefully translate into my daughter's success. So, yeah. You need it. Name it. It's yours."

His words lingered after he walked out of the door. *You need it. Name it. It's yours.* Lost in thought, Sky sat down and leaned back into her chair, steepling her fingers. It wasn't easy to make a first, or second impression, but Remington Kneeland was doing a damned good job of it.

# Chapter 10

Sky opened the door to Charlie's room and found Remington asleep in a chair. The upper half of his body was draped over her bed while his head rested on his forearms. Over the past couple of weeks, it wasn't unusual for her to find him like that. Day after day, as he waited for any sign of improvement, that was where Sky found him—right by his daughter's side.

He obviously loved Charlie with all of his heart, and his devotion is what dramatically changed Sky's opinion of him. Remington was a hard man, but this situation had humbled him. She supposed it would humble any person. Still, Sky had had a chance to see him at his most vulnerable. His inability to wave a magic wand and make everything better was clearly difficult, especially since that was how he seemed to solve most of his problems—maybe not with a wand, but definitely with a phone call—except when it came to dealing with Bella. She drove him insane. There was still a lot of passion there. Sky wondered if maybe they had unfinished business.

It wasn't often Sky was able to have an unguarded moment with Remington. Watching him sleep when his facial features were relaxed was sobering.

*I wonder what his lips would feel like on mine.* Sky almost choked. She couldn't believe the wayward direction her mind was going. She *could* not and *would* not lust after her patient's father. She was a doctor, not some . . . *whatever the word was for watching people without their permission.* There was a reason she was in Charlie's room, and it wasn't to ogle her father.

Sky moved as quietly as possible over to her chart so that she wouldn't wake him. There were a couple of things Sky wanted to discuss, but they could wait until later when he was awake.

Out of the blue, Remington spoke. His voice was raspy from sleep. "Any change?"

Sky jumped a little and placed a hand over her heart. "You startled me."

"Sorry. I didn't mean to scare you."

"No need to apologize." The intensity of his gaze caused a flutter in her stomach. Sky took a deep breath. The way she had been feeling lately around him had unnerved her. Without even trying, Remington seemed to be awakening something deep inside of her that Sky hadn't even known existed. It wasn't all physical. She wished it were. Sex was easy. Emotional entanglements were not.

Remington asked the question again. "Is there any change?"

Sky cleared her throat. "Every day, her vitals are getting stronger."

"Will we be able to wake her out of the induced coma soon?"

"If she keeps improving."

Remington rolled his shoulders. "This waiting is killing me."

"I can only imagine." Sky had an idea. She placed Charlie's chart back on the wall. "Might I offer a suggestion?"

"If it's to go home and get some rest, no. I've heard that suggestion and million times, and for the millionth and one time, I'm not leaving my daughter."

The edges of Sky's lips lifted into an almost smile. "I think we all have figured that out."

His eyes narrowed. "Wait. Was that an almost smile, Dr. Kirby?" Remington wasn't sure if Sky even knew how to smile.

"A smile?" She removed it from her face. "Definitely not a smile, but maybe a smirk."

"A smirk?"

"Yeah, something that resembles a smile but isn't exactly one."

Remington had to admit it was better than her judgmental looks. They ate at him more so probably because of the guilt he was already carrying. "Okay, we'll go with a smirk. So, the suggestion?"

"Right. Well, you look like a man who works out, and we have a gym for the physicians on the top floor of the hospital." Sky tilted her head from side to side. "If you knew someone with a few connections, they might be able to get you access."

He was surprised at her suggestion. It wasn't as if they had any real conversation outside of Charlie.

His hesitation made Sky second-guess her offer. "Or, not."

"No. I'm just surprised you would suggest it. I think it's a great idea."

"Blame Charlie that I did. She brings out my good side."

"Okay, now, that's a real smile."

"I'll never admit to it." Sky liked the way they bantered back and forth.

Remington was already thinking about how good it would feel to get in some exercise. "I *could* work out and still be close to Charlie."

"Exactly. She will need you in tip-top shape when she wakes up."

"A good run would definitely help release some tension. I think I'll take you up on your offer."

"Great." Sky checked her watch. "I have another patient to see, but I can meet you by the elevators in about fifteen minutes."

*****

Sky entered the empty gym with Remington following close behind. At least she *thought* it was empty until Noah walked out of the locker room. He spotted her immediately and made a bee-line directly for them.

She could see his mind making connections where there weren't any as he looked between her and Remington. His grin had mischief written all over it. There was no way to avoid him, and it took no time at all before they were standing face-to-face. He leaned in to kiss Sky on her cheek, but she reared back just in time so that he caught nothing but air. "Hey, babe."

Noah played it off with a little laugh. "If I had known you were coming up for a workout, I would have waited for you."

Sky hadn't talked to Noah since the disastrous meeting a couple of weeks ago. She started to move past him, but he continued to block their path. "I think we got the timing exactly right. So, if you'll excuse us."

He didn't move. His look was hard as he stared at Sky for no less than three seconds before speaking again. "I see you're still angry." Noah turned his attention to Remington. "Women. They certainly can hold a grudge unlike us. We can separate the differences between personal and professional. Anyway, I've put the messiness of that meeting behind me."

Remington remained silent and watched the interaction between them. The tension was thick. They apparently had more than just a professional relationship. He wasn't interested in getting into the middle of a couple's squabble.

Sky refused to allow Noah to get a rise out of her. "Grudges are for people who hurt you. I don't think about you—*at all*—as in never."

Noah's jaw clenched. His anger was building, but he wasn't as good at hiding it. "Bringing non-personnel individuals into the gym is against hospital policy."

"As a matter of fact, I do believe sleeping with nurses in your office is too. And trust me, I have the receipts to prove it. So, you really don't want to go there." This time, Sky pushed past him. "*Again*, please excuse us."

Pissed and embarrassed, Noah attempted to grab her by the arm. "I'm not—"

He didn't get to finish his sentence. "No. You don't get to do that." Remington growled as he caught Noah's hand in mid-air. He held it in an iron grip causing Noah to wince in pain. "What you are not going to do is get physically aggressive with Dr. Kirby. Surgeon's hands are essential, and I would hate to crush yours. She has asked you nicely to keep it moving. So, I suggest you do that before this situation spirals out of control real fast." Remington hadn't wanted to get involved, but the asshole left him with no choice. When it appeared that Noah got the message, Remington released him.

Noah's face was completely red as he stepped away from Sky. He glared at her. "We'll talk later." Angrily, he marched past them and out of the gym.

Sky turned apologetic eyes to Remington. "Sorry about that."

Remington wanted to release a bit of tension, but fighting wasn't how he wanted to do it. "You okay?"

"I'm fine."

"Something about the guy has always bothered me."

"Let's just say he's a much better physician than he is a person." If Remington only knew the whole of it, he would want to do a lot more than just hit him. He'd probably want to kill him. "Anyway . . ." Sky pointed. "You can change your clothes in the men's locker room over there."

Remington nodded as they moved in opposite directions.

*****

69

For the better part of an hour, Remington and Sky ran side by side on the treadmill in silence. Since they were alone, the only sound in the gym was the hum of the machines and their feet making a steady beat when they connected with the tread.

Out of the blue, Remington spoke. "What was that earlier with Dr. Bridges?"

"A mistake I wish I'd never made."

"*Ah.* An ex. One reason why I've given up romantic relationships."

"You too? Considering I have serious trust issues, a track record of picking the absolute worst men, and my insane work schedule, I've absolutely decided to give up romantic relationships."

Remington chuckled. "You might have to do some work convincing Dr. Bridges of that."

"You know what's really insane about the entire thing?"

"What?"

"He doesn't even really want me. I've never understood the male ego."

"It's not just the male ego. I would venture to say it is just egos in general. Bella's was a doozy. When I asked for a divorce, she lost her shit. Not because she loved me, but because she wasn't sure how to spin it to the press."

Sky was shocked. She had read about their divorce in the tabloids. It had been messy. "I thought she asked for the divorce?"

"*Nah*. It was me. I didn't care how the machine spun it. I just wanted out. I was miserable, she was miserable, and I was tired of pretending for the cameras."

"If you don't mind me asking, what went wrong?"

"Bella is an actress on and off the screen. She can turn into anyone and be whoever she needs to be to get what she wants. I met her at a charity event. She blew me away. I fell hard and fast. The woman had me thinking she really cared about finding a cure for Alzheimers. A disease that affects my mother."

"I-I'm really sorry to hear that." Sky's heart went out to him.

"Yeah, me too. Long story short. She was more interested in my pockets and my influence than me as a man. Found out shortly after we were married that she could care less about the disease and lacked even a hint of compassion for my mother. After the third movie and third affair with her co-star, I was done."

"It took three times for you to be done? You have a high tolerance for pain and forgiveness."

"I would do anything for Charlie. Including forgiving her mother."

Sky had never met anyone who was willing to sacrifice for someone other than themselves. "Were you close to your parents?"

"Yes.  Very.  My parents are still alive.  I don't know how my father does it, but he has stayed devoted to my mother for 52 years.  Her disease has progressed to the point that she doesn't remember us, but he still visits her every day and brings along a single red rose."

A lump formed in Sky's throat.  "That's the most romantic thing I've ever heard.  It sounds like something from a movie.  Are you telling the truth?"

He laughed.  "No reason to lie.  I came to the conclusion that the kind of love my parents have is rare and impossible to duplicate.  If I can't have what they've got, I don't want anything at all."

"You're fortunate to have had them for role models when it comes to relationships and love."

"It didn't help me in any of my relationships.  I take it you didn't have any role models?"

"No.  I can't say I've ever seen a healthy relationship up close and personal."

"In my case, it didn't help me find one."

Silence fell between them as they continued to run.  Suddenly, Remington blurted out his thoughts as if he were exhausted from holding them in.  "I don't think I'll ever forgive myself if Charlie doesn't wake up.  I'm not sure I'll forgive myself regardless."

Sweat was dripping down Sky's face as she pressed the button to cool down.  Sky couldn't believe Remington was so easy to talk to.  They were sharing some fairly intimate details about their lives, but she was surprised at this confession. "Can I be candid?"

Remington slowed his own machine. "It's never good when a woman starts off a sentence like that. I'll probably regret saying this, but yes."

Sky patted her face with her towel. "It's obvious you are devoted to Charlie. She can feel that energy. She knows you're there. That goes a long way to help a person find their way to healing."

For a moment, Remington looked deeply into her brown eyes and saw an honesty there. Slowly, he turned away and slammed his fist down on the dashboard. "I should have fought harder. I should have been around more. I thought I was doing what was best for her."

Sky turned off her machine. "The 'what if' game is not helpful to you or her. We all make mistakes, and Charlie is going to need all of your strength."

"My daughter hates me."

"She doesn't hate you. She might be pissed at you, but hate is a hard place to get to with a parent no matter how much they suck."

"How do you know? Do you have children?"

"I don't. But I know exactly what it's like to be in a tug-of-war between two parents. I was pissed at mine for what they put me through. I'm sure you know that my father is a physician. He's also a workaholic *and* an alcoholic. As far as my mom, she didn't know she had a daughter until I graduated high-school. She went about her days constantly looking for the next man who was going to make her feel good about herself." Sky shook her head. "It was disgusting."

Remington looked on intently, listening to every word.

Sky continued. She had never shared her personal life with anyone, but given how open Remington had been, she felt she could be too. She sighed. "I was around the same age as Charlie when my parents divorced. I was so angry at them, not for all the reality-show madness they put me through, but because they didn't spend any quality time with me."

Her words didn't offer Remington a whole lot of comfort. "Given I was in China when this happened, just how is that supposed to make me feel better?"

She smiled. "Let me finish my story."

Remington put his hands up in a gesture of surrender. "Okay."

"Anyway, both of my parents, to this day, are *still* miserable souls." Sky stepped off of her treadmill and stood next to his machine, waiting for him to finish his cool down.

"I think I feel worse."

"You shouldn't, and here's why." Sky glanced up at the ceiling. "God, I can't believe I'm telling you this. They *are* a hot ass mess. Not *were*, but *are*. Yet, I still love them very much."

Remington pondered her words. "They couldn't have been too bad. You seem to have turned out alright."

"Hmm . . ." Sky thought about it for a second. "I'm not sure if that was because of them or in spite of them. They can't see past their own needs and how their parenting affected my life. Seriously, they fought so much I'm not sure how they ever conceived me."

Sky gave Remington a lot to think about *and* hope for. If he got another chance with Charlie, he would certainly make the most of it. He finished his cool down and stepped off the machine. He gave her a sexy grin. "I'll let you in on a little secret, you can have sex when you're pissed. Sometimes, angry sex is the best kind." He wasn't sure why he'd said the words. But Sky's reaction at the mention of sex was an interesting one. He couldn't tell if she was horrified or mildly intrigued.

What was he thinking? Did he really want to unlock that door if she *were* mildly interested? It not only could, but probably would, turn into an unnecessary complication that Remington didn't need. Still, he had to admit, sex was always an excellent way to release some tension. It was then that he noticed Sky in her little work-out shorts and fitted tee. She was not only his daughter's doctor, but a curvy, voluptuous, sexy woman.

At the mention of sex, Sky noticed how his sweaty white t-shirt molded to his chest. She could make out every. Single. Muscle. His washboard abs looked as if they had been sculpted from clay, and those corded muscles in his arms looked strong and capable. To put it simply, the man was ripped. When Sky realized she was staring, she quickly glanced away. She didn't know if angry sex was the best, but she had a feeling that any kind of sex with Remington would probably rank pretty damned high.

An awkwardness settled between them.

Sky needed to back away from the edge of insanity before she crossed a line. She quickly changed the subject. "I need a shower, and my legs are not only on fire but feel like jelly." She attempted a joke, and her laughter came out forced. "Remind me not to try and keep up with you."

The mention of her legs sent Remington's eyes directly to them. They were shapely and toned just like the rest of her. He wondered how they would feel wrapped around his waist. *What the hell man? She's Charlie's doctor.* He had to keep reminding himself of that. He cleared his throat and glanced away. "I should probably hit the shower too and get back."

Sky nodded.

Quietly, they walked toward the locker room. Remington thanked her. "I appreciate the workout and the pep talk."

Sky finally smiled, a real one, as she gazed into his eyes. "Anytime."

# Chapter 11

He spotted Sky sitting at a corner table in the cafeteria with her head bowed low reading whatever papers that were sprawled out in front of her. Remington's first instinct was to grab a quick bite to eat and then high-tail it back to Charlie. Then he thought better of it, considering his mood had been altered for the better since Sky invited him to workout the day before. It couldn't hurt to say a quick hello.

He moseyed over. "Do you ever take a break? I bet your soup is cold."

Sky looked up. "I guess it's a good thing that I love what I do." She spread her arm in a semi-circle, directing him to the empty chair across from her. "Please, have a seat."

Remington looked indecisive. "I should probably get back. They took Charlie to get some tests about a half-an-hour ago, and I'm not sure when they'll bring her back."

"Mr. Kneeland, Charlie is going to be gone for at least another half-an-hour. A little distraction and some lunch will do you good."

He started to decline, but Sky wouldn't let him.

"Doctor's orders."

"If it is doctor's orders, I guess I don't really have a choice. After yesterday, please call me Remington."

"Remington." It sounded good rolling off her tongue. "Then please call me Sky. Unfortunately, for you, you don't have a choice because it's definitely doctor's orders." Sky whispered conspiratorially, "If I'm honest, I could use a bit of a distraction too."

Remington took a seat. "Thanks again for yesterday. I really appreciated it."

Sky tilted her head slightly. "It was really no problem. I enjoyed the company."

"Listening to me go on and on about my problems couldn't be much fun."

Sky leaned back in her chair. "Actually, it was refreshing. It's not every day that people put down their armor and have an honest conversation, you know? There is always some imaginary wall preventing it."

Remington took a bite of his sandwich. "True. Not sure I would have had the same conversation outside of this situation."

Sky agreed. "Me either. There are very few people whom I have ever told about my parents."

He nodded. "Same about Charlie."

"You have to admit, it was way less awkward than those first date conversations. The ones that start off like '*tell me something about yourself?*' Then the person says, 'I'm *insert some fancy-smancy job title*' and name drops someone that is supposed to impress you. When what you really want to know is *who* they are, not *what* they do, and definitely not who they know."

Remington laughed. "Or how about *I like long romantic walks on the beach*. How corny is that? Not that I've been out on that many dates since my divorce, in-part because the conversations were always so tedious."

"Right! Who has time for walks on the beach? Although cuddling on the couch with a glass of red wine after a long day, sounds amazing. Or rub my feet. They hurt." Sky laughed. "I'm a show me don't tell me kind of woman."

Remington grew serious. "If I've learned anything from this experience, it is that you've got to take some time to enjoy the things that make you happy and the people you love. Life can change in a heartbeat, and you might not get the chance. Sometimes, you have just got to take that walk on the beach."

Sky didn't even realize she had placed her hand over his in an attempt to sooth him. "That's great advice." The familiar feeling of butterflies appeared in her stomach. That was not supposed to happen.

It was just for a split second, but at the feel of Sky's hand, Remington's eyes held hers. Once he realized it, he turned his attention elsewhere.

Sky quickly removed her hand.

He cleared his throat. "You know? I should probably get back."

"Right.  Me too.  I have a lot of paperwork to review."  Sky started to gather her things.

Remington picked up his trash as he waited for her.  "Don't forget what I said.  You work too hard."

Sky attempted to lighten the mood.  "Go to the beach and get a hobby."  He was right.  It was too bad she had been so consumed with work over the years, and her circle of friends was very small. There wasn't really anything Sky was passionate about outside of being a neurosurgeon, which was too bad, because after looking at Remington's lips move while he was talking, Sky was in desperate need of a distraction.

# Chapter 12

The workout Remington had with Sky helped to release some of the tension he had been carrying around. If he were honest, he could use another workout session or just some alone time with her.

Remington sat next to Charlie as he held her hand, watching and studying her face. He noticed every freckle, the soft curve of her jawline, and skin that was much too pale. He wished he didn't have to see that part of her head that had been shaved. Briefly, Remington closed his eyes. More than anything, he wished he had been a better father and hoped that Charlie would open those beautiful brown eyes and forgive him.

Sky quietly entered the room. Remington hadn't heard her. By the set of his shoulders and how low his head hung, it was obvious that he was in his own personal hell. Any parent would be, she thought. It was his voice that caught and held her heart.

"I remember when you were born. You were so tiny. You seemed like a little doll. I was afraid to hold you. Afraid . . ." Remington paused. The words seemed difficult to say. "I remember thinking my hands were too big. That they would break you." He was full of pain. "I haven't been the best father. Maybe I've even been a shitty one, but if you can hear me, I love you more than anything." Remington's voice came out as a hoarse whisper. "Come back to me, Charlie. I promise I'll make it up to you."

Sky could feel this man's love and pain. It was palpable. Something inside of her connected to this family and the ice around her heart truly began to melt. Sky had intruded on something sacred and felt a bit guilty intruding on Remington's moment with his daughter. A man as proud as him wouldn't have wanted anyone to hear thoughts that were meant just for her. Sky stepped back closer to the door. She opened it and made a bit of noise pretending to have just entered the room. She cleared her throat before speaking because it was thick with emotion. She did her best to keep it light. "Good evening. How are you two doing today?"

Remington half turned and watched Sky walk into the room. Her eyes were bright, glassy with unshed tears. "You overheard me talking to Charlie."

She wouldn't lie. Sky spoke softly as she blinked back tears. "I did hear you talking, not sure how much I heard."

"Enough to make you want to cry." He stood. Sky was close enough to touch. Remington used the back of one of his knuckles to gently wipe away a tear that spilled over. "I hope those tears are for Charlie and not me. She deserves them. I don't."

Sky stared into those incredible gray eyes, and for the first time in her life, she forgot how to breathe. They were turbulent and so damned expressive. It was as if a portal to his soul had been left open, and for a very brief moment, she was able to peek inside. There was hurt, pain and something that resembled passion.

It was as if he noticed it at the same time as Sky. Immediately, Remington shut down. He dropped his hands and stepped back. Whatever *that* was, *that moment,* it could not happen.

Sky squared her shoulders. *What the hell am I doing? I've crossed so many lines. I've got to get back on my game.* It was best if they both pretended the last minute and thirty seconds never happened. "I actually came to bring you good news. Charlie has made enough progress that we believe we can start the process of waking her up."

At first, it was as if Remington hadn't heard her. Then the upturned corners of his mouth grew so broad that it exposed the most perfect smile Sky had ever seen. It transformed his entire face. Remington's perfectly straight teeth could have starred in a toothpaste commercial.

He was beautiful.

Remington took Sky by surprise when he joyously lifted her off her feet and spun her around in a circle. "Are you serious?"

"Yeah, I am." She nodded and laughed right along with him wanting to share in his joy. For the second time, in as many minutes, Sky's mouth went dry, and her heart sped up. Being held in his arms made her tingle all over. The moment she realized it, her smile fell. *Talk about crossing lines— again.*

Remington noticed it too. Slowly, he let Sky slide down the hard planes of his body. It was only a flash of a moment, but he liked the way she felt in his arms and on his body. *Wrong time. What was he thinking? There would never be a right time.* "I'm sorry about that. I was just excited."

Sky cleared her throat. "Umm . . . no problem." *Back to business.* She scolded herself. "I need to make sure that you know what to expect. Charlie has been in a medically induced coma for a couple of weeks.

Therefore, the process that we will use to bring her out is going to take some time. It's not a snap your fingers kind of thing. It can take up to seventy-two hours or more."

Remington hung on to Sky's every word.

She continued. "Even then, Charlie may not wake up right away. If she doesn't, I don't want you to be alarmed. Sometimes, it can take the brain a little longer to realize it's awake and to start firing off on its own."

"Can you tell if there is any permanent brain damage yet?"

"Her MRI scans look very promising. I think because Charlie is so young and strong that it is helping with her recovery."

Remington appeared visibly relieved.

"I still need to warn you that until Charlie is fully awake, we will not be able to ascertain any long or short term effects from her injuries."

"I understand. This is still good news. I suppose I should call her mother." Remington ran a hand through his unruly dark blonde hair.

Sky felt a strong desire to want to do it for him. *Focus woman, focus.* "We've had someone contact her already."

"Good. That should help prevent my blood pressure from rising. Still, I'm not going to be able to think or sleep until I know exactly what I am dealing with. Now would be a good time to hit the gym."

"Well, why don't we do that?" Sky hadn't meant for the words to pop out of her mouth, but she was caught up in his excitement. Being with Remington outside of any professional capacity was not a good idea.

He responded before she could pull her words back. "I would owe you big time. You sure you don't mind? I'd hate for Dr. Bridges to find us up there again. He might start drawing conclusions."

Sky smiled mischievously. She couldn't seem to help herself. "All the more reason to go. Charlie was my last patient for today. I can meet you by the elevators in ten minutes."

*****

Remington didn't spend as much time on the treadmill with Sky as he had the last time. He needed a more vigorous workout and decided to get on the weights.

It was a cardio day for Sky. She had set her incline much too high. She was doing her best to really push herself. It was a poor attempt to ignore the presence of a man whom Sky couldn't keep off her mind. *It was stupid to invite him to work out, knowing you are attracted to him. Just pretend he's not here and get your hour done.* She coached herself. At least this time, Sky brought headphones. No more intimate conversations.

Sky listened to her favorite songs while her eyes kept drifting over to deliciousness that was Remington Kneeland.

Ignoring him was a near-impossible task. Sky looked at the dashboard and increased the speed on the treadmill. *You've got this girl. He's just a man. Remember they are like shoes.* She argued with herself.

*Yeah, but he's like the Jimmy Choo kind.* Her eyes managed to wander over to him again. Remington was pumping iron. At some point, he had pulled off his shirt to reveal a lean, sculpted frame that blew her mind. Sweat poured off his lightly tanned body. Every time he flexed his muscles, it created a mini-volcano between her thighs. Sky devoured him with her eyes as they traveled down the length of his body. Remington had that 'v' thing and a dusting of blond hair that got lost in his gym shorts.

Sky bit her lip. She almost lost her footing and fell off the treadmill.

Remington glanced up to see her faux pas. "Are you okay over there?"

Sky's face was burning from embarrassment. She held up her hand. "I'm okay. Damn shoes. Need a new pair." He'd been so focused on his workout that she hoped he hadn't seen her heated stares.

Remington wasn't fairing much better than Sky. She hadn't noticed him looking at her, but he couldn't help but admire her curves. Sky wasn't a very tall woman but more than made up for it in other areas. If she hadn't chosen to be a doctor, she could have easily been a swimsuit model. She was perfectly proportioned—breasts that would more than fit in the palm of his hands, a narrow waist and flat stomach, womanly hips, and thighs that made his mouth water. In truth, Sky was perfect. It had taken all of his strength not to just sit and watch her run on that treadmill. For any man with his vantage point, she would have been a must-watch event. Remington needed to get his mind together. He absolutely should not be thinking about Sky Kirby that way and felt like a pervert sneaking glances.

It had been much too long since he had been with a woman. And given his circumstances, it should have been the furthest thing from his mind. But with Sky less than ten feet away and looking like a siren, she was making it difficult. Maybe instead of fighting it, Remington should welcome the distraction.

The moment of truth was coming regarding Charlie's condition, and it filled him with nervousness and dread. *What if she didn't wake up?* So far, running and lifting weights hadn't been able to quell his energy. Remington got up off the bench and added more weights to the barbell. It wasn't a good idea since he didn't have a spotter but he needed to bring his anxiousness down to normal levels *and* get his mind right.

Sky, on the other hand, was running herself into exhaustion, trying to get her libido under control when she heard a voice in her blue-tooth earpiece. "Sky. Why have you been avoiding me?"

That's what paying attention to her sexy patient's father did to her. It caused a lapse in thought and had Sky answering a phone call before checking the display. "Mom." Her forced jovialness might have been a bit too much. "I haven't been avoiding you. I've just been really busy with work."

"Sky Kirby Johnston. I know you. You've been avoiding me."

"I would never do that." The sarcasm dripped from Sky's lips.

"I'm going to be in town this weekend and wanted to get together for dinner. There's someone I want you to meet."

"Is this a new fiancé?" Sky said half-jokingly.

Omara Johnston-Reid-Hall remained silent.

Sky looked heavenward. "Mom? You've got to be kidding, right? Please don't tell me that you are gunning for husband number four?"

"Then I won't share my good news with you. I'll wait and share it on Saturday when you meet Sam." Omara laughed nervously.

"Mom!"

"Be happy for me, Sky. I think he is the *one*."

"The ink from your divorce is barely dry on husband number three! You *know* I've only ever wanted your happiness, but you won't find it like this."

"Sam is different. He used to be a minister."

Sky was shocked. She stopped her machine before she actually did fall off. "Are you serious!?"

Remington heard Sky and looked over. Whatever was going on, she looked horrified. He placed his barbell back on its stand and sat up from the bench.

Sky's mom was still talking in her ear. "Of course, I'm serious. I take the institution of marriage very seriously and would never play around with something like this."

*So serious that it's your sixth engagement and will be your fourth marriage,* Sky thought. "He's a minister." Sky said it as if she were talking to a small child. "You don't even go to church. What denomination is he? Do you even believe in God?"

"He's the denomination of God. That's all that matters. Anyway, that's neither here nor there. And don't be so negative. If I'm happy, you should be too."

Sky was truly speechless.

"Please, honey. Be happy for me. And . . . gotcha!"

"So, you were just kidding?"

"About Sam being a minister? Yes. He's really some big-shot Hollywood agent. But not about getting married."

Sky shut her eyes and pinched the bridge of her nose. "Mom, I have to go. I have *an* . . . *um* . . . something came up. Can I call you later?"

Sounding none the wiser that Sky's head was about to explode, Omara responded. "Of course. Call me later tonight."

Sky hung up.

"Is everything alright?" She opened her eyes to find Remington standing close.

"I'm fine. Just remind me to never get married and never have children."

He scratched the side of his head as he joked. "Just the kind of woman I'm looking for. Seriously, you look like you could use a punching bag."

"I could."

"There isn't one, so how about some weights?  You can take your frustrations out on the weights instead of whoever you were talking too.  It'll help release the aggression in your eyes."

"A punching bag would be perfect."  *With my mother's face on it.* She thought.

They walked over to the free weights area.

Remington picked up a couple of ten-pound barbells and handed them to her.

"Ten pounds?  Really?"  She lifted an eyebrow.

"It's not how heavy they are. It's the repetition.  You don't have bulky muscles, so I figured a little something for the aggression and a little something to tone.  Squat like this."  He pulled her back to his front and placed his hands on her hips.

His touch warmed her.  As he spoke into the back of her neck, the heat from his words spread throughout her entire body.

"Feet braced apart, like so."  *Focus, Rem.  Forget how damn good she feels in your arms.*  Remington was fighting the same internal battle.

Sky tried hard to listen and to follow his instructions.

"Now, pretend like you're about to sit in a chair."  His voice was low, husky.

"Like this?" She didn't recognize the sound of her own voice. The heat from his closeness fell off of him in waves, the strength of his arms, the natural smell of his body caused her to turn slowly into his arms.

Sky's eyes connected with his, and Remington held her gaze.

She couldn't breathe as time stood still.

The moment his gaze traveled to her lips, a kiss was inevitable.

Sky wasn't sure who moved first, but his lips touched hers in a soul-stirring, heart-pounding, panty-wetting kiss.

# Chapter 13

Sky dropped the weights. They landed somewhere on the mat behind them.

Sky felt a rush of passion pool between her thighs as his hot tongue traced the outside seam of her lips. Remington nipped at her bottom lip with his teeth before sucking it into his mouth. She gave Remington full access as he thrust his tongue fully inside. Skillfully, he explored her, and Sky explored him too.

Their tongues swirled around each other as they struck a rhythm that was both urgent and needy.

Sky melted against him and let her hands roam free. She placed them all over his hot and sweaty chest touching him in ways she had only fantasized about.

Remington moaned into her lips.

Time and space no longer existed. The world shrank to just the two of them.

His hands slid lower and gripped the back of Sky's thighs urging her to lift and loop them around his waist.

Her mind was no longer in control—her body was—and it did what it was told.

He was hard. Real hard. She felt the length of him as he squeezed her ass and ground into her sex. Sky couldn't help but rock into him.

The ache for more was making her crazy as the pulsing between her thighs intensified.

Remington continued to thrust into her mouth and stroke her sopping wet core.

Sky sucked hard onto his tongue as she dug her fingers into his hair and completely gave herself over to the pure feelings of ecstasy.

She didn't know how he managed it, but Remington dropped to his knees while never breaking their kiss.  He laid Sky back onto matt.

She cradled him firmly between her legs.

The sound of their kisses and their heavy breathing echoed throughout the room.

Sky could feel the heat of his chest through her thin t-shirt.  When he cupped her breast, that was when she broke the kiss.  *Sensory freakin' overload!*

Sky spoke through gasps.  *"God, Rem . . . This. You. Too much."*

He rocked hard into her as he spoke into Sky's neck.  "Not nearly enough."

Her nipples were hard and begging to be lavished with wet kisses as he squeezed and kneaded them.  Hell, she wanted him to kiss her all over her body and wondered what his tongue would feel like tasting her clit.  The mere thought made Sky crisscross her legs around his waist again and roll her hips into his cock.

He growled into her neck as he kissed his way down the soft column and lower. "We have on entirely too many clothes." His hands were everywhere. Remington managed to take off Sky's shirt and unhook and remove her bra before she even realized it. When he latched onto a tightly pebbled nipple and sucked, Sky arched up off the matt. She squeezed her eyes shut.

*Holy, shit. I'm going to die. He feels so good. Maybe I've already died.* Sky thought.

"Is everything okay in here?"

They froze. Sky started to freak out and unhooked her legs. Frantically, she looked around for her t-shirt. She found it and crushed it to her breasts.

"Is everything okay in here?" The voice asked again.

Sky couldn't form words. She was on the edge of a full-on panic attack.

Remington was calm. He responded for her. "Everything is good." The heat in his eyes hadn't diminished with the appearance of another person. Remington caressed the side of Sky's cheek. "Real good." The second part of his answer could only be heard by her. She licked her bottom lip that was still swollen from his kisses. Remington sat back on his haunches and slid his hands down to her waist, resting them there. From the look in his eyes, there was no doubt that he wanted to finish what they had started.

Sky inhaled deeply getting some much-needed oxygen to her brain. She looked around Remington to see Henry Moss, a security guard that had been with St. Lucia's Hospital for over twenty-five years, looking at them suspiciously. Flustered and still trying to control her breathing, Sky answered, "We're fine, Mr. Moss. Mr. Kneeland is my guest. We were just getting in some exercise."

He had that fatherly tone in his voice. "Exercise, huh? On the floor? Okay."

A hint of laughter snuck into Remington's eyes.

"Y-yes. Mr. Kneeland was just showing me a few things." Sky was still attempting to cover up their full-on make-out session.

Mr. Moss chuckled to himself. "I'm sure he was," he said sarcastically. "Just a gentle reminder the gym closes at eight—even for staff members and their *guests*."

Sky nodded. *Duly chastised.* "Got it. We were just about to hit the showers."

"Uh-huh." He didn't sound as if he believed them.

Remington couldn't keep the smirk off his face. His back was to the guard which was probably a good thing. He'd hate to embarrass Sky any further by sporting a full hard-on and exposing the naked breast that was still wet from his kisses and not hidden by her t-shirt.

Remington hoped his large frame kept her out of view. A bit of possessiveness took over. He didn't like the thought of other men looking at her. He turned slightly to make eye contact with the guard. If the twinkle in his eye was any indication, it was apparent the man had seen more than Sky would have liked.

Henry moved to leave. "Oh, by the way, Dr. Kirby?"

"Yes?"

He laughed lightly as he walked out of the gym. "Don't forget security cameras are everywhere in this building. So, if you're planning to do something you don't want to be seen, the locker room should work. Just make that *shower* fast. I'm off the clock in the next thirty minutes."

Mortified, she bit her bottom lip and smiled. "Got it. Thanks, Mr. Moss." After he had gone, Sky wrinkled up her nose. "And that happened."

"I like the way Mr. Moss thinks. Shower?" Remington was still hard as a rock.

"I think—" She paused. "We got a little carried away." Sky attempted to move out of his embrace.

Remington tightened his hold. "I don't think we got carried away enough, and there's an easy fix to that." He bent low and placed a kiss on Sky's lips.

She started to melt into him again, but the consequences of having sex with Remington fell over her like a ton of bricks. Mr. Moss was an example of that. Her job, her reputation, and everything Sky worked hard for would be at risk. Gently, Sky placed both hands on his chest and pushed. Her body was screaming *are you crazy,* but common sense had to prevail.

"Henry probably just saved us from making a huge mistake. We can't do this."

Remington wasn't ready to give up. "Not only do I think we can, but I promise it'll be *you can't walk straight for a week* kind of good."

Sky trembled. "I am sure you could make good on that promise. But tomorrow is a big day for both of us. I don't think we should, nor do we really want, to cross this line. Your daughter's physician can't be sleeping with her father."

She was right. *Dammit. Score one for common sense.* Remington released his hold on her but, even knowing she was right, there was still something inside of him that didn't want to let go.

# Chapter 14

Sky entered Charlie's hospital room to find her lying very still with a serene look on her face. She wasn't as pale as she had been a couple of days ago. As a matter of fact, she looked like a replica of sleeping beauty. Too bad it wasn't as easy as a prince kissing her on the lips to wake her up. It had been three days since they stopped using the medications to keep her in the coma, and Sky was beginning to worry that Charlie hadn't regained consciousness. "It doesn't make any sense." She spoke softly to herself as she reached for her chart. Sky couldn't understand it. All of her test results looked good, and they were getting stronger every day. Charlie should have woken up. The MRI showed there was brain activity and most all the swelling had gone down from her spinal cord injury. Even though there was not a way to determine the extent of any brain damage until she woke up, *If* she woke up, nothing on paper could account for why she hadn't.

Sky checked and double checked her medical chart.

Bella had finally shown up after being MIA for the past couple of weeks. She hissed loud enough for Sky to hear her from the other side of the door. "What am I supposed to do, Remi!? Am I supposed to wait forever? Charlie might not ever regain consciousness! If she does, she'll need around the clock medical care. Kane and I are in no position to give her what she needs."

Another argument—round one or maybe a thousand. Every time they were in the same room, there were fireworks. Sky tried to ignore them.

"You're her goddamned mother! Charlie can feel your presence. Or, in this case, your absence. You're supposed to be here. Charlie's not a pet. You can't just come around when it's convenient!"

*You have a point there,* Sky thought.

"I'm being realistic. Kane and I can't abandon all of our other responsibilities!"

"What other responsibilities? It's not like you're promoting a movie. You are living off my dime! What's the difference between living off of my money from the comfort of the home I pay for or this hospital? Charlie needs you here, not chasing Kane all over the goddamned world."

Sky saw movement on Charlie's face. Although her eyes were closed, they twitched, which wasn't all that unusual. Only, it looked more like a blink, as if she were reacting to her parents arguing. When a slight crease formed across her forehead, Sky started to wonder if Charlie was still under.

She remained quiet as she observed the girl's reactions.

Bella couldn't contain her anger. "Why does it always come back to money?"

"Because it's my money!"

"Regardless. Kane is none of your concern. But if he has to leave the country, I'm going with him. He has obligations."

Sarcasm dripped from Remington's lips. "For argument's sake, let's pretend he has a real job. If I can run a billion-dollar corporation from this hospital, then so can he."

Sky wanted Kane to leave. Something in her gut told her he was the cause of Charlie's injuries. Then the guilt hit her. It was never too far away, considering she and Remington were in this weird sexual place—almost like they were in a holding pattern—*waiting*. Sky had never told Remington about the bruises or her suspicions. *What if I were wrong? But what if you were right?* The thought turned her stomach.

Bella was still putting on an award-winning performance. "Like I said, what Kane does or doesn't do is none of your business! You should be happy, singing from the rooftops even, that I've made this decision. So, I don't understand why you are fighting me. You've always wanted custody of Charlie. I'm giving it to you."

"Physical custody, not legal, but I plan to change that."

Those words caused Charlie's face to scrunch up as if she were in pain.

Sky saw it. Slowly, she placed the metal chart back into the holder on the wall above the bed. Charlie was awake. She was pretending to be unconscious. Sky wasn't one hundred percent sure and decided to test her theory. "I had parents like them. They drove me nuts."

Charlie didn't respond. She didn't move at all.

Sky continued. "I know it might seem easier, but you can't hide forever." Moments of silence ticked by. Sky didn't think she would answer.

She didn't know if it were even possible for her to respond, but then Charlie spoke. She didn't open her eyes. Her voice was hoarse, a raspy whisper, from not using it over the past few weeks. "They wouldn't care."

*Excellent. She remembers her parents' fighting in the past and how it makes her feel.* A positive sign for her cognitive responses. Sky made a mental note to write that down in her chart before sitting on the edge of Charlie's bed. She continued to watch her intently. "It might not seem like it, but that's not true. I'm sure both of your parents love and care about you very much."

Charlie didn't respond.

Sky pushed a little harder. "What do you remember about them?"

Moments passed. "They hate each other, and sometimes they hate me." Charlie said it matter-of-factly. Then she asked, "Can I have some water?"

Sky's heart went out to her. She knew that *I don't care routine* all too well. "How about some ice-chips instead?"

Slowly, Charlie nodded.

Sky went over to the table that had ice in a little bucket. She scooped some up in a cup and walked it back to Charlie's bed. She placed an ice-chip on her lips and rubbed it across before allowing her to take a small one inside her mouth. "We're going to have to take even the ice chips slow, okay?"

"Okay."

"Good.  Where was I?  My parents divorced when I was about your age.  It was hell.  If I were honest, it was hell while they were together.  Your parents don't hate you.  They just have to figure out how not to take their issues with each other out on you.  My parents never learned that lesson.  To this day, they can't stand to be in the same room.  If they can't learn to do better, there is still good news!"

Charlie's eyes remained closed.  "Like what?"

"You won't always be twelve, which means . . . One day, you'll be able to move out on your own and live the kind of life you want.  You can visit with your parents as much or as little as you like."  *Hopefully, after this accident, they'll learn to put you first.*  Well, Sky knew that, at least, Remington was willing to do it.

Charlie's eyes fluttered open.  She had trouble focusing.  Everything was blurred.

Sky took out her light pen and shined it in Charlie's eyes for an examination.  "So, how long have you been awake?"

"Since last night."

"*Hmm* . . . You did a good job of convincing the nurses you were still asleep.  Do you remember what happened that caused you to be here?"  Sky asked the question as if it were no big deal.

Charlie tensed up and touched her neck with her hands.  "My throat hurts, and I-I . . ." She hesitated.  "I don't remember."

Sky didn't believe her for a second. Her body language proved she remembered something unpleasant. An *accident* would have been unpleasant, so that could be it too. Sky wouldn't push. But she had to admit, Charlie's reaction only added fuel to her suspicions. "That's okay. I'm sure everything will come back to you soon." Sky quickly changed topics. "I can see that you have feeling in your arms. Can you lift them for me?"

Charlie did as she was asked. "I'm so hungry."

Sky was happy to see she had mobility in her upper body and that she had an appetite. "No food for you yet, but maybe some chicken broth?"

"Whatever." Charlie's speech was good even though it was a bit slurred.

"Let's finish this first. Can you follow my fingers?" Sky lifted her forefinger and slowly moved it from side to side. Charlie appeared to be following along.

"So, again, how'd you manage to pull off being unconscious?"

"I slowed my breathing when the nurses came in to check on me."

"I see. You have the gift too, huh? Do you want to be an actress like your mom?" Sky pulled out her percussion hammer and went to the foot of Charlie's bed.

They could still hear them arguing outside her door. Charlie's voice was a barely-there whisper. "I don't want to be anything like my mom."

Sky hated that she felt that way about her mother, but hell, Sky sometimes *still* felt that way about her own. The difference was that Sky accepted the fact that her mother was flawed and loved her in spite of it. Charlie hadn't reached that level of maturity. She lifted the covers and ran the edge of the little triangle up and down Charlie's left foot. "Can you feel that?"

Charlie whispered, "What?"

"Hmm . . ." Sky mimicked the same action on the other foot. "How about this?"

Charlie was beginning to freak out. "I don't feel anything. Are you doing something?"

"It's okay. Nothing to get worked up over." Sky tried to soothe her. "Remember, your body has gone through a major trauma. It's still trying to heal itself. Everything might not be working like it's supposed to just yet, but that doesn't mean it won't."

"But I can't feel anything below my waist." There was panic in Charlie's eyes.

Sky glanced up and gazed into the beautiful chocolate depths of a scared little girl. Sky wasn't known for her bedside manner, but she smiled and tried to exude warmth. "That's not unusual, and as I said, sometimes it takes a while for everything to get back to normal."

"You don't have to sugarcoat it. Tell me the truth. I can't feel anything? Does that mean I won't ever walk again?" Charlie spoke with much more wisdom than her age should allow.

"Do you want to? I mean, walk again?"

Charlie nodded vigorously. "Yes."

"Then focus on that. The mind is very powerful." Sky covered Charlie's legs back up with the blanket and lightly patted her thigh. "Now, should I go get your parents?"

Nervously, Charlie looked at the door. "Is it just my mom and dad? Is anyone else out there?"

"As far as I know, it's just the two of them." Alarm bells were ringing, and red flags were waving. Sky did her best to conceal her concern. She plastered on a smile. "According to the doctor-parent handbook, I'm required to get them."

Charlie's face relaxed as she exhaled. "Then I guess I have no choice."

# Chapter 15

Sky stood with Charlie's most recent CT and MRI scans in her hands. "Damn."

"Another late night?" Nia popped her head into Sky's office, carrying little white boxes of Thai food.

"Unfortunately, yes and another long day to go with it." Sky sighed.

"Figured. I brought dinner to you and a six-pack of beer since you canceled."

"Sorry. I've just been bogged down." Sky was able to muster up a tired smile. "I knew there was a reason I love you. But you know I can't have alcohol when I'm on the clock."

"I figured, technically, you were off the clock since you're never really on the clock."

"That's that lawyerly talk. Anyway, what brings you to the hospital this late?"

"You. If I don't make sure you eat when you're in this mode, you will starve. How is she?" Nia pointed to the scans as she took a seat at Sky's desk. "Charlie Kneeland, right?"

"Yeah." Sky put the scans to the side and took a seat opposite Nia. "As far as her brain injury, there is a bit of short-term memory loss, but for the most part, her cognitive functions are returning to normal. It's her spinal injury that has me worried. She's been in therapy for close to a week, but so far, she can't feel the lower half of her body. Based on these new scans, she seems to miraculously be healing nicely. I don't get it."

"Maybe it'll just take a bit more time." Nia served the food on paper plates and handed one to Sky.

"Maybe." Sky was still pondering what she could do or have done differently.

"You've really taken a personal interest in her. Does Remington Kneeland have anything to do with that?"

Sky looked up from her plate. "Why would you ask that?"

"Oh, I don't know." Nia shrugged. "Maybe because since you met him, you've been walking on sunshine."

"My moods have nothing to do with Remington." *Not completely anyway,* Sky thought. "This case is just . . . Charlie reminds me so much of myself when I was younger."

"Oooohhh . . . That's got to be terrifying." Nia laughed.

Sky laughed too. "Shut-up. I was an amazing kid."

"Amazingly terrible." Nia slowly turned serious. "I want to meet him."

"Who?"

"The man who has done the impossible and turned you inside out."

Sky still looked thoroughly confused.

"He's captured your attention, and that is no easy feat. He deserves a medal just for that alone. Any more workout sessions?" Nia took a bite of her own food.

"First, I don't know what you're thinking, but Remington is the father of my patient."

"I think you need to get laid, and you said you were mildly attracted to him."

Sky had forgotten that she had told Nia that part. *Thank God I didn't tell her the really juicy parts,* she thought. "Second, even if I were mildly attracted to him, things are crazy at the hospital right now. I have to be three times as good as my male counterparts, some of which can barely stitch a wound, to gain just a modicum of respect. It would be nearly impossible if I were caught doing something like sleeping with my patient's father."

"You have admitting privileges at most of the hospitals in Chicago. With your experience, you could practice at any hospital in the country. Screw them if making you feel small makes them feel better." Nia munched on her food. "Anyway, back to the deliciousness that is Remington Kneeland. I saw what he looked like on the internet. If I had a snowballs chance in hell of hooking up with him," Nia snickered, "I wouldn't mind doing some things that might damage my reputation."

Sky listened to Nia drone on and on about what she would do with Remington. Sky smirked as she thought about that incredible kiss they had shared in the gym. The mere thought made Sky's body heat up.

If Nia only knew that Sky had already done a few things any respectable woman who cared about her career would never do, but she decided to keep that bit of information to herself.

# Chapter 16

Sky walked into the rehabilitation room to find Charlie at a station where she was half-seated in a wheelchair-like contraption and, with the help of staff members, was pulling herself up onto two very long but stationary poles. Charlie's face was flushed and showed her focus and determination.

She was working hard to exercise. The muscles in her upper body were weak but functioning. The lower half of her body, on the other hand, where she still did not have any feeling was more challenging to exercise.

Sky tucked her hands in her white lab coat. "Wow. Look at you. At this rate, you'll be ready for the Olympics in no time." Sky smiled as she rooted her on.

Charlie's hair had fallen in her face, and she tried to blow it away. "I'm following your advice."

"What was that?"

"You said the mind was very powerful and to focus." Beads of sweat had permeated across her brow, and Charlie's voice was strained. "Mind over matter, right?"

"*Mmmhmm.*" Sky watched her intently. She turned to the physical therapist. "How long have you guys been at it?"

He shrugged. "About twenty minutes. We were just about to wrap it up."

Charlie whined. "No. I don't want to stop yet. I can go a little longer."

"You know? I didn't realize until just this moment how much you remind me of your father." Sky crossed her arms across her chest.

Charlie's expression changed as she sat back down in her wheelchair. Her voice was low. "I'm nothing like him."

"Really? I see a brilliant and determined young woman. Your dad showed that exact same determination the entire time you were unconscious. He never left your side. If I didn't know any better, he probably willed you back to this side of heaven."

"My dad?" Charlie paused. "Was here? With me? The entire time? My mom said—" She cut off her words.

Sky didn't want to speak out of turn but also wanted Charlie to know the truth. "From what I understand, your dad was on a plane within minutes of finding out you were hurt. He even called and harassed me from China, and once he got here, I know for a *fact*, he never left your side."

Charlie laughed. "Harassment. Now *that* sounds like my dad. What did he say to you?"

"He asked if I was the best neurosurgeon around. When I said yes, he still called in the top surgeon in this field to double check my work. Your father literally did not leave this hospital until you opened your eyes. My guess is the only reason he is not here now is because he's setting up your rehabilitation after-care for when you are released."

Charlie's face fell. "I won't be going home with him?"

It was clear that Charlie loved her dad just as much as he loved her. "Maybe. Not sure how the rich and famous people do it. There are facilities specifically to rehab your type of injury. It is probably costly to set it up in someone's home. From what I know of your dad, he can do it. Do you *want* to go home with him?"

Charlie's eyes were cast downward. "I guess," she sighed. "Maybe I am a little tired."

Speaking of the devil, Remington strode into the room, carrying a bouquet of red roses. Everything about the man screamed confidence and swagger, *including his walk*. Sky's breath caught at the sight of him. Her pulse quickened. *Down girl,* she chided herself.

Charlie noticed that something caught Sky's attention, so she followed her line of sight. *Interesting*. She thought. Charlie pushed her suspicions to the side. Surprisingly, given her complicated feelings with her father, Charlie had to admit that her heart lifted the moment she saw him.

"Hey, kiddo." He bent low and dropped a kiss on her forehead. "These are for you." Remington handed her the flowers. When he stood, he acknowledged Sky. "Dr. Kirby."

"Mr. Remington." It was funny that only a week ago they were tearing each other's clothes off. Now, they were using each other's surnames. "I was just checking on my favorite patient."

He smiled at Charlie. "Isn't that a coincidence? She's my favorite patient too." Remington tilted his chin to the therapist. "I can take Charlie back to her room."

Sky decided it would also be an excellent time to give the father and daughter some alone time. "Well, I have a couple more patients to see, and then I'm off to my office to complete some paperwork. It's going to be a long night." She started to leave.

"Dr. Kirby . . ." There was a part of Remington that didn't want her to go. But he knew spending quality alone time with Charlie was imperative. They needed to rebuild their relationship. "I'm in the process of making some rehab arrangements and would love to get your input."

"That's fine. I'll be available in a couple of hours and will probably be here until seven or eight tonight. Just drop by whenever you have some time."

"Okay, that's good."

"Okay, great."

They stood, staring at each other in awkward silence.

Sky broke eye contact first. "I had better go. See you later, Charlie." Sky waved as she walked away.

Remington couldn't tear his eyes away from her until she had left the room.

Charlie wrinkled her nose. "You haven't dated in a while have you?"

"What? What are you talking about?"

"Dr. Kirby. If you like her, you should just tell her. I think she might have a thing for you too. Maybe ask her out on a date."

Remington pushed Charlie toward her room. "What would make you say something like that?"

"Oh, I don't know. It could be the goo-goo eyes you were making at each other."

Remington chuckled. "First, I don't make goo-goo eyes. Second, my only concern right now is you."

Charlie turned serious. "Dr. Kirby said you haven't really left the hospital since I got here."

"She said that, huh?"

"Yes. Is it true?"

Remington wheeled Charlie into her room then picked her up out of her chair. She wrapped her arms around his neck. It wasn't a tight hold but enough for him to want to dance for joy. Remington did his best to keep his emotions intact and gently placed her on her bed. "I was exactly where I was supposed to be, and I'm sorry that I haven't been around more."

Charlie wasn't expecting that—an apology. Her eyes welled up with tears, but she fought them back.

"There isn't any good excuse for not being there for you like I should have been. I want you to know that it wasn't because I didn't love you—

because you own my heart. Stupidly, I thought I was doing what was best for you. Little girls your age need their mothers."

"That was stupid," Charlie whispered. "Little girls need our fathers too."

"Duly noted." He kissed her on the side of her head.

Her tears started to fall. Remington used the back of his knuckle to wipe each one away.

She touched her forehead to his. "I love you too, Daddy."

They stayed like that for a while. Pulling away from her, Remington nervously rubbed the back of his neck. "What do you think about living with me for a while?"

She stared at him. "Mom doesn't want me?"

At that moment, Remington hated Bella and the damage she was doing to Charlie. "It's not that. Your mother only wants the best for you. She's just afraid that she won't be able to give you what you need."

"I heard you two arguing. I know she gave you physical custody."

"You heard that?"

"I did. If she would rather be with Kane instead of me, then let her. I don't need her."

Remington's heart was in a vice. "You know that's not true."

"It is true." Charlie sighed. "I wish Mom were more like Sky."

"Why do you say that?"

"She's honest with me. She doesn't do things that will hurt me or sugarcoat things. Sky treats me like I matter."

"You do matter. You matter to your mother and me. I hate that you have to find out like this that your parents are human and have major flaws. Bella is just scared. When things frighten her, she doesn't know how to deal with them, and sometimes, her choices are not ideal. Some of my choices haven't been the best either."

Charlie hadn't thought of it that way. "Dad? Are you happy?"

Remington had to think about it. "You make me happy. So, yes."

"What if I never walk again?"

"You are still you. Nothing will ever change my love for you. If you never walk again, we'll figure it out. You'll still have an awesome life. I'll make sure of it."

"Sky said if I focus on my health then walking again is possible, but I have my doubts, and I don't want to let anybody down."

Remington tucked Charlie's hair behind her ear. "There is nothing you can do that will let me down. It seems like you and Sky have become really close?"

"Yeah. I like her. I like her a lot. You should ask her out. Maybe she can make you smile more. After you divorced Mom, you stopped smiling." Remington hadn't realized it and certainly didn't think Charlie would have noticed.

"I don't know." He shrugged. "Not that I'm contemplating dating anytime soon, but she's pretty focused on her career right now." If he asked Sky for sex, he thought she would probably say yes. A date? He wasn't so sure. "Do you think she would say yes?"

"Absolutely! You might be flawed, but you're a catch."

Remington thought about his daughter's words. There she was lying in bed recovering from a horrible accident, and yet she was thinking about him. "I meant it when I said my only concern right now is you. Speaking of . . ." He was careful with his words. "We haven't really talked about the accident. Charlie? What happened that night?"

The sparkle in her eyes dimmed. "I-I don't remember." She made a big show of her yawn. "I'm so tired, Daddy."

Something told him that that wasn't true. He would be patient for now, but eventually, Remington wanted the truth.

# Chapter 17

"Knock-knock." Yolanda stuck her head inside the door. "Can I come in?"

Charlie woke up, and her smile grew wide. "*Ohmygosh*! What are you doing here?"

She walked through the door. "Not only is it me, but I also brought a friend." Yolanda pulled Charlie's favorite doll from behind her back and handed it to her.

"La-La!" Charlie reached for her and held the doll as if she were a delicate, priceless artifact.

"Yep." Yolanda smiled broadly. "She missed you, and so did I."

"How did you get here?"

"Someone once told me that you'd be surprised what a hundred dollars could convince people to do." Yolanda giggled.

"You paid a hundred dollars to come see me! That's a lot of money."

"Girl, are you crazy? I took the bus." Yolanda full-on laughed and embraced Charlie in a hug. "Oh, I'm sorry. Am I holding you too tightly?"

Charlie's eyes filled up with tears. "I'm fine. My legs don't work, but if I'm honest, I've never been better."

"Oh."

Charlie held La-La close to her chest. "Don't be sad. My dad is here, and now you and La-La. For the first time in a long time, I think things are looking up."

"Your dad?"

"Yes. Can you believe it? He came as soon as he heard and hasn't really left my side. Well, except to take a shower and change clothes. I think he's worked out at the hospital gym. For the most part, we've been talking through our issues, and when this is over, I'm going to live with him." Charlie's face beamed.

Yolanda sat down in shock. "Whoa. That's fantastic!" She looked on sadly. "Don't get me wrong but you going to live with your dad means we won't be staying in the same house anymore. That's a bummer, but I'm happy for you. I'll miss you."

Charlie's smile brightened even more. "No, you won't because I'm going to ask if he'll bring your mother on as one of his staff members." Charlie looked down at the lower half of her body. "I'll need a lot of help."

"If you could pull that off, it would be amazing. But . . . aren't you going to miss your mom? I mean, I know you too have your differences but—*she's your mom*."

Charlie's lips tightened. Her face hardened. "No. I won't miss her."

Cautiously, Yolanda asked, "What they're saying happened to you in the paper, is it true? You didn't really fall off that horse, did you? What did Kane do?"

119

Before Charlie could answer, her father returned fresh from a shower. "Yolanda?"

"Yep. It's me."

"Look at how you've grown since the last time I saw you. It's really good to see you."

"You too, Mr. Kneeland."

He glanced around. "Where's your mother? I haven't seen Sophia in a while either."

She answered nervously. "She's not here, Mr. Kneeland."

"Where is she?" Remington used the towel hanging around his neck to finish drying his hair as he eyed her suspiciously.

"She's . . . *um* . . . at home."

"So, how did you get here this time of night?"

"The bus."

"You took the bus from the estate to the city? Your mother wouldn't allow that. It's too dangerous. Okay, here's what we are going to do. Visit with Charlie for a few more minutes, since I've got a couple of calls to make. Then grab your stuff, and I'll take you home."

*****

Remington pulled through a set of familiar gates to a place that he had called home for almost ten years. It was the first time he had been back in three. In the beginning, his visitation with Charlie had been contentious.

Eventually, they had worked out a plan. When it was his turn to have Charlie, Remington would have a car pick her up and take her to his private plane. There, she would meet up with his assistant, Ashleigh. She was typically their go-between.

As he drove toward the house, Remington didn't have any feelings nostalgia. It was more like dread.

Remington didn't have any qualms about leaving or divorcing Bella. Not one. Well, maybe one. He never should have left Charlie behind. He should have, at the very least, bought a home closer. Maybe if he had, she wouldn't be in the hospital learning how to live a very different life than what he had planned for her. In his defense, Remington hadn't wanted to uproot her from the only home she had ever known. Dealing with divorcing parents was difficult enough. It was worth it to him to pay over a hundred grand a month if it meant his little girl could hold on to a piece of normalcy.

"Thank you for giving me a ride home, Mr. Kneeland."

He had almost forgotten Yolanda was sitting in the passenger seat. "No problem. I hope I won't have to remind you again that taking the bus to the city at your age is dangerous."

"No, sir." She nodded. "I can't believe I did the same thing that I told Charlie not to do the night she was injured."

"What? What was Charlie planning the night she was injured?"

Yolanda started talking to herself in Spanish. *"Oh, God. I promised. Me and my big mouth."*

She didn't realize Remington was fluent in Spanish. "You promised what? What happened that night, Yolanda?"

Her eyes widened. "I said I wouldn't say anything."

Remington's chest began to feel tight. "I don't know how to help Charlie if I don't know what really happened."

She thought about it for a moment and decided it was best to be as honest as she could without betraying too much of Charlie's trust and jeopardizing her mother's job. "Charlie had planned to run away. She was having some problems at school and was afraid of how Mr. and Mrs. Langston might react to her getting kicked out." Yolanda left out the details about the abuse.

His voice had an edge to it. "Why was she afraid of how they might respond? Should she have been scared?"

Yolanda's eyes were downcast. "I don't know, Mr. Kneeland. I just know she wanted to leave. I can't tell you anything else."

Remington inhaled deeply then blew it out slowly. He didn't want to scare the child, but if there was something nefarious going on, he needed to know about it. Something in his gut told him something other than the story he had been fed happened that night. Remington didn't want to come across as too much of a hardass. He attempted to soften his voice. If there was more information to be gleaned from Yolanda, the whole flies and honey analogy came to mind. "Thanks for telling me what have. If you remember anything else, or if there is ever something you need . . ." He reached into his inside suit jacket and handed Yolanda his business card. "Call my assistant, Ashleigh. She'll get in touch with me."

Slowly, Yolanda lifted her head and one corner of her mouth ticked up into a small smile. "Thanks, Mr. Kneeland."

"No problem." His rental car rolled to a stop in front of his former home. Yolanda's mother was standing outside in her uniform, wringing her hands. As soon as Yolanda exited, she received a tongue lashing in Spanish.

As Remington stepped out of the car, Sophia spoke. "I'm sorry that my daughter bothered you, Mr. Kneeland."

"Yolanda is not a bother. She's a good kid. If I'm honest, I should have thought to ask if she wanted to visit sooner since the girls have always been close. It did Charlie good to see her."

"REMI?!" He saw Bella walking toward them as she sang his name.

*Dammit.* His goal of making a quick exit was foiled.

"Goodnight." Sophia and Yolanda moved quickly to enter the house.

"How is Charlie?" Bella asked.

"You would know if you spent more time at the hospital."

"Don't start." Her voice softened as she ran a finger up and down his arm. "We just got back into town last night and were recovering from jet-lag."

One minute Bella hated him. The next, she was unabashedly flirting. *The woman was mental,* he thought. Remington ignored her and used the back of his thumb to scratch the side of his head. He asked the question that had been on his mind for weeks. "Bella, what happened the night of the accident? Why was Charlie out in the wee hours of the morning?"

She wrapped her arms around her body. "There is not much more to the story than I've already told you. She fell off the horse."

His voice began to rise. "She had no damn business out that time of night to begin with. Something is not adding up."

"Why do you always look for more to a situation than there is? If you don't believe me, then ask her."

The rage in his chest was about to burst out. Remington clenched his teeth. "She doesn't remember."

Kane came bounding out of the house and down the stairs toward them. He was pissed. "Remington. What are you doing at my house?"

"Your house? Are you fucking kidding me?" The prick had a lot of nerve. "I suggest you take your ass back inside before I lay you out where you stand."

Bella got in-between them. "*Now, now*, boys. No need to be fighting over me." She ate up what she thought was their jealousy for her. "Remington was just asking about the accident."

"If your daughter hadn't been out chasing the security guard by the stables for a midnight rendezvous, maybe none of us would be in this situation!"

"What?" Remington saw red.

"Yes. Your precious angel was trying to hook up with a man almost twice her age. In her effort to show off for him, she fell off the damn horse."

"Is that true?" Remington glanced at Bella.

She blushed. "She's just a child, Remi. She probably thought she was in love."

Remington glanced from Kane to Bella. He didn't for one second believe a word that came out of either of their mouths, but if he didn't want to get brought up on murder charges, it was best to leave. And that was precisely what he did.

Remington got into his car and slammed the door. His tires squealed as he peeled out of the driveway.

He made a mental note. *Call the lawyers. Put the damned house up for sale.*

# Chapter 18

"I just got your text. What's up?" Sky walked into Charlie's room the next morning.

Charlie struggled to sit up on her own but managed. "I was hoping you would come before my dad comes back from the cafeteria. Can I talk to you about something?"

Sky pulled up a chair and sat down. "Of course."

"I mean, you have to promise not to say a word, especially to him."

"As long as it doesn't put you in danger, I'll take it to my grave." Sky crossed her heart and gave the Boy Scout salute.

Charlie pursed her lips together. "I am a little nervous about moving in with him."

"*Okaaaay*. Would you rather live with your mother?"

"Oh, god. No!" Charlie wrinkled up her nose.

Her reaction went a long way to confirm Sky's suspicions.

"It's just that I've changed a lot in three years. What if . . . What if, he doesn't like me?"

"Are you saying that you haven't spent time with your father in three years?"

Charlie shook her head. "No. I spent Father's Day, his birthday week, two weeks out of the summer, and spring break with him. Both my parents travel too much for the *every other weekend thing*. When it was his time to have me, he was always busy working. He left it to his assistant to keep me busy." Charlie sighed. "Who am I kidding? Now that I think about it, I'm sure that's what will happen when I move in. He'll hire a glorified babysitter. I guess I've answered my own question. Too bad my legs don't work. At least, I could have run away. I can't even sneak out anymore."

Sky chose her words carefully. "I have a feeling that your father is going to try to make some changes in his life. I think he knows that he made mistakes with you, and more than anything, probably wants a chance to do better."

The door to Charlie's room opened, and there stood Bella in all her pageantry glory.

"Dr. Kirby, isn't it interesting that you think you know my Remi so well, enough to advocate on his behalf." She strutted further into the hospital room in full red-carpet attire. "Hi, darlin'." She floated over to Charlie and kissed her on the forehead as if she hadn't been MIA. "How are you feeling today?"

Charlie didn't make eye contact as she mumbled. "Okay."

Slowly, Sky stood. *She did not like that woman.* Bella was a self-absorbed, vapid piece of work. But for Charlie's sake, Sky would play nice. "Charlie is showing marked improvements every day. At this rate, she could be released to a rehabilitation center very soon." *If you were around more, you would know that.*

"Okay? Just okay? How am I supposed to go to this industry thing tonight if my baby-girl is feeling *okay*?" Bella had never been more animated.

Charlie turned her head toward the wall. "It's never stopped you before, so I don't know why today would be any different."

Bella's porcelain white face turned three shades of red. Before she could respond, Remington sauntered into the room carrying a bouquet of balloons. Sky was in his line of vision, and his grin grew wide the second he saw her.

For a brief moment, Sky's eyes locked with his, and then she remembered they weren't alone.

Bella saw the exchange, and she did not like it. "There you are, Remi!" Her high-pitched voice was all sweet like saccharine.

It made Sky want to vomit. She also realized Bella was the reason she hated the name Remi.

The smile on his face faded as soon as he realized Bella was in the room.

Sky attempted to make a graceful exit. "I have a few patients to see."

"Oh. Good. I was starting to think Charlie was your only patient." Bella's words were full of venom.

Charlie squealed. "Mom! Stop. *Pleassse.*"

Remington's voice joined Charlie's as it hardened. "Stop with the shenanigans, Bella."

Sky wasn't in a Michelle Obama kind of mood. But out of respect for Charlie and Remington, she wouldn't go low and snap. Instead, she focused on Charlie. "It's fine. I'll see you later." She wasted no time leaving.

*****

Sky was elbow deep in paperwork when Bella entered her office. "We should have had a conversation a long time ago. Since we didn't, now is as good a time as any. It's obvious that I need to set a few ground rules."

Sky looked up, placed her elbows on her desk, and linked her fingers together. "Pray tell, what would those rules be, Mrs. Langston?"

Bella wasn't used to people not kowtowing to her. *She was an Academy Award Winning Actress—Bella damn Lord-Langston.* And she planned to make sure Dr. Kirby recognized it! Her eyes narrowed. "Stay out of my family's business. If you can't, *or won't*, don't think because you're fuckin' my ex-husband that I don't have the power to have your ass replaced!"

Sky was deathly calm as she spoke. "Just so you understand, threats don't work on me. They usually have the opposite effect, and for the record, who I'm sleeping with is none of your business."

"Maybe I need to be a little clearer. If Remi wants to sleep around with any old thing, that's on him. *My* priority is Charlie. You need to know that you've only remained her surgeon because we needed you in a pinch. She's awake. *We* no longer need you."

Sky leaned back in her chair and steepled her fingers together. "Really?"

"Really.  So, if you want to continue to get all of this positive press coverage at the expense of my daughter, follow the damn rules.  Otherwise, this little career you're trying to build might become a casualty of my wrath."

"Since we are being brutally honest, you should know, the only rules I follow are my own and certainly not the ones of a has-been aging actress, trying to hold on to her youth.  If Charlie was *really* your priority, you wouldn't pop in and out of her life like she was a pet.  Where the hell have you been these past weeks?  Furthermore, why was she out at three in the morning and even in a position to harm herself?  Chasing whatever you are chasing, you are failing her.  There is not a movie, a script, or anything in this world that would take priority over my daughter's well-being."

"Bitch, you don't know me!  Don't you dare try to tell me how to be a parent."  Bella was ready to jump over Sky's desk and punch her.

Sky wasn't finished.  Her eyes narrowed.  "I see you *clearly,* and the only priority you care about is yourself." Sky sat up on the edge of her seat. "Another thing, I'm Charlie's physician because I'm the best at what I do.  I'm in the media because I'm making history about things that actually matter.  Long after you stop getting movie offers and awards, I'll still be using my Harvard and Johns Hopkins educations saving lives.  As a matter of fact, up and coming doctors will learn how to be better doctors from my work."

Bella placed both palms on Sky's desk and leaned in slightly to make sure she heard her every word. "You really don't want to mess with me. I can crush you like a bug."

Sky stood, placing her palms on her desk. She leaned toward Bella as they stood face-to-face. "I'd like to see you try."

The stare-off lasted for seconds but seemed like an eternity. Sky would die before she blinked first. Fortunately, she didn't have to. Bella lifted her chin slightly, then turned and left.

# Chapter 19

Sky opened the door and stepped out onto the roof of the hospital.  It only took a moment for her eyes to adjust to the darkness.  She spotted him sitting alone with his legs dangling over the side of the building like it wasn't an insurance risk—or something Sky hadn't done a million times herself.  She walked over to him.  "Hey.  I got your text?  You wanted to meet on the roof?"  After her run-in with Bella, Sky debated coming.

"A little birdie told me this was a great place to collect your thoughts."  Remington turned around to see the woman who had been haunting his dreams.  "Is that a six-pack of beer?"

Sky lifted it a little higher.  "Actually, it's a five-pack."  Even though Remington made her feel things she shouldn't, Sky was glad she made the decision to meet with him.  Just being in his presence made everything else going on in her life fade into the background.

Sky rambled.  "My best friend bought it a few days ago.  I put it in my office refrigerator.  It's missing a bottle because *she* had no problem downing one.  I can't drink while I'm on duty. Fortunately, I'm off.  Anyway, I figured you could use a cold one—or two." She took a seat next to him and let her legs dangle over the edge of the wall.  Fortunately, there was a ledge below, so if for some reason they tipped over, they wouldn't fall thirty stories to their death.  She handed him a bottle.

"I mistook you for a wine type of woman."  Remington twisted the cap off and turned the bottle up.  He took a long pull.  "Just what I needed."

"I am. But, every now and again, nothing beats a nice cold beer." Sky took a drink from her own bottle.

Remington seemed lost in thought. "It really is nice up here. It's like another world where problems don't exist. Thanks for telling me about it."

"It's peaceful. It's gorgeous in the early morning, but more so at night. When I don't have time to go home, sometimes, I'll come up here to recharge my batteries." Sky continued to admire the night. She sighed. "Speaking of home, when was the last time you left this hospital?"

Remington raised an eyebrow. "I should be asking you that same question."

Sky shrugged. "There is a difference between us. It's just me. I don't have anyone that depends on me. You, on the other hand, do. You need to take care of yourself so that you can care for Charlie."

"Maybe you should try to change that *it's just you thing*. I guess my little speech about *the walk on the beach* didn't register."

"Funny you should say that. I'm *still* looking into rescue dogs, trying to find the right one. I hear they love long walks on the beach." She laughed more to herself than him. "Seriously, until I find the right partner, I might as well make myself useful here at the hospital. But back to you, you never answered my question. When was the last time you left this hospital?"

"Months. Home is in Phoenix, and I was in China for a while. But to answer your question, I left the hospital today to shower at the hotel I'm paying for but never sleep in." As much as Remington fought it, he enjoyed Sky's company, which was why he had broken down and texted her.

Remington knew he was asking for trouble when the words left his mouth, but he couldn't seem to help himself. "I didn't know you were looking for a partner?"

Sky pulled her lower lip into her mouth before answering. "I'm not looking per se. But if the right man came along, I might be willing to re-think some previously held positions."

His eyes followed the small action of her lips. "Positions like no marriage and children?"

"Maybe. I'm sure I was being a little dramatic that day when I said that. My mother can bring out the worst in me. At some point, I want a family. However, the man I'm with would have to be really incredible for me to even consider either of those things."

Remington glanced out into the darkness. "Being a parent is the hardest job in the world. My situation makes dating almost impossible. Not sure if I would be able to figure out how to balance the time. Charlie really needs me. It's been difficult to be away from her even for a second."

"I bet. Charlie's amazing." Sky got the message loud and clear. He didn't have any space in his life for her. It was more than understandable.

Maybe if things were different, Remington would pursue Sky. He rationalized his wanting to spend time with her as just a way to keep a good relationship with his daughter's physician. But Remington couldn't ignore the fact that when they were together, Sky had been able to do what no one else had in a long time—make him feel at peace even in the midst of madness. Speaking of peace, he could win a Nobel Prize for keeping his hands to himself over the past couple of weeks. Even though he had been conflicted about what he wanted, it didn't matter since Sky had put the kibosh on anything romantic between them. Sometimes, the glances that passed between them made him think she was also conflicted about the nature of their *friendship*. There was no rationalizing the fact that friends don't typically make a man's body ache, and Sky had his in a state of semi-arousal every time they were together.

Sky realized she had been friend-zoned, maybe even doctor-zoned. So, there was no need to test the waters about her desires. Being both, she needed to act accordingly. "As a physician, I can't stress how important it is for you to take care of yourself. Thus, the beer."

"You're worried about me?" He said it as a joke, but his eyes told another story as they looked into hers. They were so intense and filled with need.

He wanted her—*physically*. She wanted him too. Sky wondered if she could handle being in just a physical relationship? Would she be okay with that? It would solve both of their problems.

Sky began to wonder if he could see the secrets she kept hidden deep inside the longer Remington held her gaze. *Could he tell that underneath the workaholic armor was a woman that wanted more?* And by more, she meant him.

She broke away from the heat of his gaze and attempted to put things back on track. Remington had just told her that he couldn't pursue a relationship. *Sex?* That was a different story. There were so many reasons not to indulge in any kind of relationship with Remington, not the least of which was her fear that he could make her fall in love.

Sky needed to keep things light and away from that imaginary line they kept crossing. "Of course, I am concerned. I worry about all of my patients."

"I'm not your patient. Charlie is."

That was the problem. Reality was rearing its ugly head *again*. Charlie *needed* to be the center of his attention. Remington took another pull on his beer and glanced up into the inky night sky. He marveled at all the twinkling lights.

Silence stretched out between them until he spoke. "Charlie's never going to walk again is she?"

Sky had to be honest. "I don't know." She spoke quietly. "It can take some patients weeks to feel anything and others months. So, don't give up hope."

"I suppose I should just be grateful she's alive. She's lucky to have you fighting for her. But . . . damn it. Charlie is a young, vibrant girl, and she might never get to experience her first high school dance. What really kills me is that one day, I won't be able to walk her down the aisle."

Sky placed her hand flat on his back and rubbed it across. She bent low enough where they were face-to-face. "Let's say that her nerve damage is permanent. That won't prevent Charlie from having a full and exciting life, including you walking her down the aisle."

Weren't those the same words he'd just uttered to Charlie? Remington stared at Sky long and hard as he thought about her words. As if his body had a mind of its own, he bridged the mere inches of space between them and pressed his lips to hers.

Initially, her body stiffened, thinking about all the reason why kissing Remington wasn't a good idea then she relaxed. For once, Sky didn't want to think. She wanted to do what felt right.

Her heart was beating so fast she thought it was going to burst out of her chest. The electricity flowing through her body was indescribable, and she wanted to feel like this forever. Sky snaked her arms around his neck in an effort to bask in all the sensations he made her feel.

Remington's voice was hoarse. "I've tried, but I can't stop thinking about you."

Breathless, Sky responded. "Me either."

His plan which was no plan at all was only to kiss her. *One kiss. We can get it out of our system*. Gently, Remington pushed Sky down against the gravel of the rooftop. He dragged his tongue over her lips. His need to taste Sky and deepen the kiss was overwhelming. "You have no idea how much I want you."

"About as badly as I want you." She could absolutely understand. She needed this, needed him.

He plunged his tongue into her mouth and kissed her with all the pent-up frustration brimming within him. He wasn't sure how long it lasted—a moment, an hour, forever? He just didn't want it to stop. He couldn't stop. What was supposed to be one kiss had turned into much, *much* more. It was like a locomotive had left the station. There was no stopping it.

Remington broke the kiss and used his tongue to lick the side of Sky's exposed neck and shoulder. His hands were busy too as they caressed the soft curve of her inner thigh forcing her skirt up. He eased his body in-between her legs, and Sky cradled him there.

The huge bulge in his jeans made contact with her engorged sex. Sky rolled her hips into him, creating a friction that sent electricity throughout her entire body. She recaptured his lips with hers, kissing him hard.

Remington knew what her body was crying out for. His was singing the same song. He wouldn't allow this to go that far. As much as he wanted to be buried to the hilt in her body, he wouldn't cross that line. Sky wasn't built for just a sexual relationship. He promised himself he would stop before things got too out of control, but he would try to give her as much relief as possible.

Remington continued to explore her body with his hands. He squeezed them between their bodies—on a mission, searching and seeking until he came in to contact with a lacy barrier.

*Eureka.*

"*Mmm.*" Sky moaned and arched up into his hand.

His eager fingers found their way to the swollen seam of her pussy lips through her panties. He trailed his fingers up and down, repeating the motion over and over again each time adding a bit more pressure.

Sky was a soaking hot mess. Her panties were useless. The throb at the apex of her thighs turned into a full-on ache. She needed some relief.

When Remington came into contact with the edge of her panties, he hovered around it for just a moment before slipping a finger underneath.

"*Ahh.*" Sky closed her eyes, threw her head back, and gasped unable to catch her breath. In that moment, coherent thoughts were far, and few but one came to mind. *If this is my reaction to the touch of his finger, I'm going to die the second he enters me.*

Sky felt like silk. He watched her breasts heave up and down. He watched her beautiful face and what it looked like as he pleasured her.

She was so damn responsive. Her reaction to him made Remington stop just to admire her.

Her eyes popped open. She looked worried. "Is something wrong?"

Voice heavy and laced with passion, he responded. "Nothing could be more right."

Sky noticed that his eyes were now a darkened gray as they looked into hers. "Then don't stop." She was needy. Her hips bucked up into his hands *and* his dick, knowing that they were the key to her satisfaction.

She begged. "*Pleeease.*"

Slowly, Remington parted her tender flesh with one of his fingers and plunged it deep into her soft, wet core.

Sky's eyes rolled into the back of her head as she arched her back and clamped on to him.

*God, she was sexy.* He continued to watch her. He reveled in her soft moans while her fingers dug into his arms.

Remington pulled his finger out, only to add another digit when he plunged back inside her liquid heat. He allowed his fingers to do what he knew his dick couldn't. As much as he wanted Sky, Remington promised himself he wouldn't go there. For now, he would take pleasure in her pleasure. That was his plan until she placed a nice little love bite on his neck and began to unbutton his jeans.

Sky slipped her hands inside. He wasn't wearing underwear, so it was easy to fist him. He felt like silken steel. He was also so large that she could barely wrap her entire hand around him.

Sky stroked him from the base to the tip and back down again.

His pre-cum leaked onto Sky's fingers. She used her thumb to spread it around the tip of the bulbous head of his cock and continued to pump slowly at first, then faster and faster.

He returned the favor. She stroked. He thrust inside her body. They alternated until the pleasure was too intense.

Whatever idiotic promises he made to himself about not fucking the shit out of her were out the window. He pulled his hands away from Sky and started to remove her underwear.

Her breathing was labored.  She wanted him with every fiber of her being then remembered they were on the roof.  Anyone could come up.  Sky released him.  "My apartment is less than twenty minutes away."

Her words jarred him back to reality.  Remington placed his forehead against hers.  It was hard getting air into his lungs.  "I can't leave.  I promised I wouldn't, at least, not yet."

Disappointed, Sky closed her eyes.  "I understand."

Remington's phone announced a caller.  "Charlie is calling."

Their moment was over.  It vanished just as quickly as it happened and reality came crashing down.

Remington rolled off of Sky and sat up to take the call while she adjusted her clothing.  "Hey, you.  I'm here.  I just stepped out to get some fresh air."  Remington looked apologetically at Sky.  "Okay, I'll be down in a minute." Seconds later, he disconnected the call.  "I've got to get back."

It took a minute, but Remington buttoned up his pants, then stood and held out his hand to help her up.  Her eyes were bright, glassy, and it killed him.  He was doing this to her.  He knew she wanted more than he could give.  Remington was going to have to cut the bullshit.  He couldn't keep doing things like this simply because he wanted her near.

"Of course." Sky got to her feet and smoothed out her skirt.  She was only slightly embarrassed that she had been rolling around on the roof of the hospital.  Fortunately, she was sure there were no cameras up there.

He squeezed her hand because he hadn't been able to let it go. "From now on . . ." He glanced up. "Every time there's a perfect night like this, I'm going to call it Remington's Sky." His lips barely touched hers in a feathery light kiss. He sighed. The battle was over. It was impossible to do what he knew he needed to. "There are a million and one reasons why we shouldn't get involved, but right now, I don't give a damn about any of them. Things are crazy. I don't have to explain that to you. It's selfish and wrong of me to ask you to be patient. Still, I'd like to figure out whatever this is between us."

Sky smiled and whispered, "I'd like that too." His words made her knees go weak. They were exciting and terrifying. What was she supposed to say, considering he had just named a sky after her? The rational response would be *pursuing a romantic relationship was not a good idea*, but when Sky imagined taking the long walk on the beach, it was with Remington.

Maybe it could work-out somehow? Sky couldn't help but think *things that are impossible are only impossible until they weren't*.

*****

Remington watched Charlie sleep while his mind kept fantasizing about Sky. The woman had his mind playing tricks on him. It was a no-brainer that he was physically attracted to her. Any warm-blooded man would be. But there was also something else that called to him on a deeper level. That was the part that made him nervous. Still, he was excited about the possibilities. Sky didn't want or need anything from him. She was a successful, thriving woman all on her own. She also had a soft spot for his daughter, and Charlie seemed to have the same feelings. Over the past weeks, the two of them developed some type of bond. That endeared Sky to him even more. Maybe when Charlie was more settled in whatever the future held, provided Sky was still single, he would invite her on a real date—show her that he was interested in more than just her body—not just stolen moments. Remington had to be honest with himself too. He was very, very interested in her body.

A very sleepy Charlie called out to him. "Daddy?"

Remington had zoned out again, thinking about Sky. "I'm here." He caressed her forehead with a feather-light touch.

"I called you and then fell off to sleep. What were you thinking about? Dr. Kirby?"

"Dr. Kirby?"

"Dad. I'm not five. You get this look on your face when you think about her."

"You are too smart for your own good." Remington moved Charlie's hair out of her face. "Let's just say you were right? What if we were attracted to each other? Would that bother you?"

Charlie thought about it. "I already told you to go for it. I mean, at first, I wasn't sure. I feel like I'm just getting you back . . . And—".

"You know that no one can ever replace you right?"

Charlie spoke quietly. "I'm learning. I also see how she makes you act silly. It makes me feel good to see you happy especially since I know you haven't been for a really long time."

Remington didn't know what to say. "You're too perceptive."

Charlie twisted her fingers together. "I like Dr. Kirby *a lot*. She's not only good for you, but she's also good for me."

Remington lifted the corner of his lips in a lop-sided grin. "Yeah? So is this about you or me?"

"I'll admit—it's about us. So, don't mess this up."

"What do you suggest I do?"

"Take her on a date."

He tilted his head from side-to-side. "Maybe when you're all better."

"That's too far into the future. You've barely left the hospital in weeks." She tipped her chin toward the chair he had been sitting in. "Sitting there can't be comfortable, and that's where you've been sleeping. Why don't you go to your hotel tonight? Or, better yet, do something special? Is it too late to take Dr. Kirby to dinner? Seriously. She is gorgeous."

"I can't disagree with you there. She's beautiful." He scratched the side of his head.

"I know right? You need to make a move and nail this thing down for us."

Remington laughed out loud. "You think so?"

"Yeah. I do. It was my dad that taught me that if you see an opportunity not to let it slip through your fingers." Charlie reached out and placed her hand on top of his. "I'll be here in the morning. I can't exactly run away." She attempted a joke.

Remington's throat was thick. "You're amazing. You're teaching me what real strength and courage look like."

Charlie blushed.

Remington felt as if he and Charlie had passed some kind of milestone. He didn't know if this was a good time but was compelled to ask the question that had been nagging at the back of his mind. Remington's voice was quiet. "Charlie, what happened the night of the accident?"

The question clearly caught her off guard. She swallowed. "I-I don't remember."

Remington knew that she was holding something back. "You know you can trust me, right?"

She bit her lip. "When it comes back to me, I promise you'll be the first person I tell." Charlie exaggerated a yawn, which he noticed she tended to do when she didn't want to talk about her accident. "I'm so tired. You should go before it gets too late. See you in the morning?"

The twelve-year-old minx was dismissing him. After a slight pause of indecision, he bent low and kissed Charlie on the forehead. "Bright and early. I'll have my cell phone with me if you need me for any reason. Okay?"

"I'm going to be asleep. Now, go. Stop stalling." She pulled the covers up to her chin.

Remington grabbed his overnight bag and threw it over his shoulder as he backed out of the room. "Are you really sure about me leaving?"

"Please leave." She rolled her eyes. "Bye, Dad."

"Okay. Okay." He put his hands up in surrender. He stopped at the door before leaving. "Your phone is by your bed. Make sure it's charged."

"Yep." She smiled sweetly. "I love you."

Remington's heart had never been so full. "I love you too."

# Chapter 20

Sky needed to calm her hot ass down. Even after a shower, her body was still humming from her time on the roof with Remington.

She attempted to distract herself as she sat curled up on the sofa in front of the television, drinking a glass of wine and flipping channels. Sky had a moment where she wished she had someone important in her life. Someone who could hold her and listen as she moaned and groaned about the trials of her day. It wasn't really *someone*. It was Remington. His face is what flashed through her mind. His life was more complicated than hers, and it was so full. He said he wanted to figure things out, but there really wasn't any room for her.

*Bzzt. Bzzt. Bzzt.* Sky reached over onto the table and grabbed her phone. A smile crossed her face as she instantly recognized the number on the display. She must have thought him up. "Hey."

He could hear the smile in her voice. "Hey." It was probably the same one she heard in his. "I've got this bottle of wine that I think you might enjoy."

"I can't wait to try it. If tomorrow is anything like today was at work, as soon as I walk through the door, I might just drink it straight from the bottle."

"Was it our rooftop experience or an all-around rough day?"

Sky sighed. "Do I need to pick one? Although the roof-top was probably the highlight of my day."

"Then how about you let me inside, and we can pass the bottle between us—maybe even finish what we started."

Sky sat up and threw her legs over the couch. "Wait. Where are you?"

"Outside your door."

She was surprised. "How'd you—"

"You don't know yet that I have my ways?" He chuckled. "Remember, I sent a squad car for you."

Sky got up and quickly went into the kitchen where she dumped her glass of wine. "But I didn't know you knew my specific address." She untied her silk scarf from her head and put it in a drawer as she ran her fingers through her wiry curls.

"Are you going to let me in?"

Sky went to the door, took two deep breaths to calm her nerves, and slowly opened it.

She took his breath away. It was only a little after nine p.m., but Remington wasn't expecting Sky to open the door in a slip-like negligée that barely came down past her ass.

She smiled saucily. "I thought you wanted to come inside?"

"You better believe I plan to do a lot of cummin'." Remington pulled Sky's body flush into the hard planes of his body and kissed her. She opened like a flower, and he slipped his tongue inside the hot cavern of her mouth. Their kiss was hot. A continuation of what they started on the rooftop.

Remington walked Sky backward into her condo and closed the door with his foot. Her hands snaked up into his hair. With his one free hand, Remington squeezed her ass into his hardness. Her moan made him want her more than he wanted his next breath. But he kept hearing the words, *don't mess this up*, in the back of his head. He tore his lips away. Breathing heavy, he rested his forehead against hers.

Sky whispered, "What's wrong?"

"Not a damn thing. I need to tell you that I've made a decision."

"About what?"

"Just to be clear, there is nothing about you that is casual. Not this kiss, or the sex we're going to have. I'm done trying to deny how I feel. I know what I want. I've decided to take ownership of you—mind, body, and soul. So, I'm going to take my time. I have all night to do whatever my heart desires."

Sky pulled back slightly. "You've decided, huh? I don't have any say-so? You think it's that easy?"

"We knew it from the moment you opened the door." Remington nipped at the soft column of her neck. It took all of his strength to slow things down. His voice was husky. "How about some more wine?"

"More?"

He threw his head back and laughed. "I tasted the merlot you were drinking before I got here."

Sky shrugged. "C'mon. I needed a drink. But once you offered me some of yours, I dumped mine. Figured yours would be better."

"Everything about me is better."

"Oh, Gawd." Sky took him by the hand and led him to her living room. "You are so full of yourself, Mr. Kneeland. You better be able to back it up."

*****

Sky sat snuggled up to Remington with her head resting on his shoulder watching a late night talk show. Actually, *it* was watching them. The volume was low and it really only served as background noise as they talked about everything.

Remington laced his fingers with hers. "Earlier, you said you had a rough day. Want to talk about it?"

Sky looked heavenward. *Are you really answering prayers this quickly? If so, I have a few more requests.* She ran her hand down his chest. "Actually, no. I don't want to introduce any negative energy here."

As if she weighed nothing, Remington lifted Sky and sat her on his lap. He cradled her cheek in his hands and brought her face inches from his. "You're beautiful."

Sky could feel the heat of his breath tickle her lips. "So are you."

Remington kissed her. "I haven't been with a woman in the past couple of months. After the last time, I had a physical. I'm clean."

Sky cleared her throat. She had always made sure Noah wore a condom when they had sex, and they both had been tested before they had become intimate. "So am I, and I'm on the pill."

He stood. "Then I think it's time."

"For what?" Sky giggled.

"For me to make good on my promise. Which way to your bedroom?"

She pointed, and Remington stood with her in his arms, carrying her. All the lights were off in her room except for a lone night-light. It cast a beautiful glow around them.

Remington deposited Sky onto the center of her bed like she was the most precious thing in the world.

Sky bit her bottom lip in anticipation as he started to remove his clothes. When he stood in front of her wearing absolutely nothing, her mouth went completely dry. She was able to find a few words. "I'm feeling a bit overdressed."

Remington crawled into bed and up her body. "You won't for long." He took her mouth in another toe-curling kiss.

He didn't lie. Remington grabbed the hem of her negligee and pulled it up over her head, tossing it somewhere around the room. Just like that, they were both naked.

He sat back a little bit so that he could stare at the beauty spread out before him. Tenderly, Remington ran his thumb across her bottom lip. "You're so beautiful. You can't imagine how long I've thought about making love to you."

"Probably not nearly as long as I have."

He could see the honesty in her eyes, and it completely destroyed his restraint.

He kissed her hard on the lips. Sky's eyes fluttered closed. She relished the feel of his touch when his hands began to travel up her ribcage to cup her breasts. She wrapped her arms around his neck as he kissed each one. But the little volcanic eruptions between her thighs came when he pulled a tight little bud into his mouth. He made love to it just like she knew he was going to make love to her body. He swirled his tongue around her nipple and then sucked hard. The sting made Sky's back bow.

"I'm not sure which one of your breasts is my favorite. It'll take some time to figure out." Remington made sure to lavish her other breast with the same attention.

He used his knee to prompt Sky to open for him. She spread her legs wide as he moved their bodies, so that he lay between her thighs.

His cock was pressed up against her entrance. Sky was anxious to feel him moving inside of her and couldn't stop squirming. Every time she moved, it triggered a pleasure so intense that it caused her to lose her breath. The feeling was so delicious that her body wanted more and began to move uncontrollably on its own.  She had to stop before she lost her chance.

"Wait."  Sky quickly switched places with Remington and straddled him.  She had been fantasizing about this.  She slid lower and lower until his shaft and her lips were almost touching.

He felt the heat of her breath on his cockhead.  Remington completely lost the ability to breathe on his own.  When Sky pulled him into her mouth, he felt that he had most assuredly had been transported to heaven.

Sky couldn't wait to taste Remington.  She sucked the length of him into her mouth inch by excruciatingly slow inch until she reached the base of his dick.  Then she sealed her mouth closed around it.

Heaven was too small a place for where Remington thought he'd landed.

It took a moment for Sky to adjust to Remington's size.  He was so large it took all of Sky's concentration to breathe through her nose and flatten her tongue.  She started to move.  She ran her lips up and down, squeezing his girth with her hand and mouth.

*"Shit. You . . . Sky."*  Remington couldn't form one complete sentence.  He slid his hands into her thick dark hair as she picked up the pace.

He pulled his bottom lip into his mouth and bit it as he watched her work.

Sky raised up on her knees, but her elbows were anchored just outside of Remington's hips. It forced her ass in the air. She looked up at Remington watching him watch her as she stroked him up and down with her wet mouth. The heat in his eyes made her pump faster and faster.

Remington held her head cradled in his hands so tightly that every time she pulled back it stung. She loved it. As a matter of fact, his heated gaze and the pinch of the pain were the hottest things she had ever experienced.

It caused her own core to spasm and beg to be filled.

Remington pulsed against her tongue, and she tasted his pre-cum. *"Mmm. So good."*

The vibration of her words was almost enough to drive him over the edge. He knew if she kept it up that he would lose it. Somehow, Remington managed to disengage Sky and flip her over onto her back.

"I wasn't finished." She said in a husky tone.

His mouth met hers again as he nestled himself at her entrance. "The first time I cum needs to be inside of you."

Remington grabbed hold of his shaft and slid it up and down the crease of Sky's entrance. She was dripping wet.

Her body was clenching at air until Remington began to ease forward inch by excruciating inch. The grip Sky's body had on him was tight as she squeezed and pulsed around his hardness. *Damn, hot and tight. The perfect combination.*

154

Sky moaned and lifted her hips.

Remington couldn't take it any longer and surged all the way inside until he was deeply embedded within her body.

Sky cried out.

He pulled back, then thrust forward again, finding a frantic and hurried rhythm.

Sky dug her nails into his back. Her head thrashed from side to side as he pounded into her. The sound of him sliding in and out of her body, the headboard crashing against the wall, and her screams of his name was going to have the neighbors looking at her crazy, but Sky didn't care. Being with Remington was worth a little crazy.

He continued to fuck her senseless. He pumped in and out hitting her g-spot every time. Sky was building toward an orgasm the likes of which she had never experienced. Remington hooked one of Sky's legs over his shoulder and adjusted his angle for even deeper penetration.

*Was it possible to die from pleasure?* Sky thought it might be.

The sound of him slapping against the back of her leg with each and every stroke also found Remington close to exploding.

*"Oh, God!"* Sky grabbed handfuls of her sheets and clenched them in her hands.

Remington could feel the beginnings of her orgasm. He thrust hard, ramming in and out of her. Sweat was glistening on both their bodies.

"Shit!" He cried out. He felt himself tighten. He couldn't hold on any longer and reached between them to rub Sky's clit.

She exploded. She squeezed her eyes shut and allowed wave after wave of orgasmic bliss to wash over her. It was not only the best orgasm she had ever experienced but also the longest.

Seconds later, feeling her clench around him, Remington growled and released his seed deep within her body.

After he emptied ever last bit of himself, he gently lowered Sky's leg and collapsed next to her feeling wholly and completely satisfied.

It took a while before their breathing got back to normal. Eventually, it did. While they were still feeling the euphoric effects of their lovemaking, Remington pulled Sky into the crook of his arm and rested his chin on her shoulder.

Moments later, they were both asleep.

# Chapter 21

Noah didn't bother to knock when he entered Dr. Shaw's office. "Have you heard? A reporter just called me for a statement. The shit is going to hit the fan in the morning."

He responded. "I heard. I am working on a plan to minimize the damage."

"There is only one way to limit the hospital's exposure, which if we handle correctly, will also help us with our Sky Kirby problem."

Dr. Shaw looked up from his computer screen. "Let's not pretend like this won't save you from having to stand before the medical board."

"There is that." Noah didn't see any point in denying it. "Who would have leaked the information to the press?"

Shane turned accusatory eyes toward him. "My guess is Jazlyn Farrow."

"Jazlyn?" Noah genuinely looked surprised. "Why would she?"

"Because you can't keep it in your pants." Shane was pissed. "I can't keep cleaning up your messes, Noah."

Noah ignored his remark. "I don't see how it benefits her to leak anything."

"She hates Sky. It's low hanging fruit. Jazlyn came to see me about a week ago about filing a harassment report against her. She claims you and she have a consensual sexual relationship, and when Sky found out, she retaliated against her since she also has a *thing* for you. Sky is a lot of things, but I highly doubt she would do something like that. I considered allowing Jazlyn to file the report as a way to get Sky out of my hair, but screwing Sky would also screw you, and more importantly this hospital, so I talked Jazlyn out of making a claim."

"She's lying. You should fire her."

"On what grounds? That she's a liar? *Right.*" Shane rolled his eyes. "Underestimating these women is going to cost you. Do you honestly think Jazlyn doesn't have emails, texts, and more to back-up some of her claims?"

"It's impossible. It never happened."

Shane was skeptical. "So, you weren't sleeping with her?"

"I mean, yes. I was but—"

"Then, at the very least, she could create a scandal. If you haven't noticed, I'm already in the middle of cleaning one up."

Noah rubbed the back of his neck. "What are we going to do? It could potentially come back on me?"

"I'm having Sky's emails scrubbed, and I just need you to sign this." Shane handed him a pen and pushed paperwork in front of him.

"Those are not my notes. They are Sky's." Noah hesitated.

"Do you want to keep your job?"

He wasn't going down over that Kneeland girl. Noah reached for the pen and signed his signature on the bottom line.

Shane smiled. "Great. Now, all that's left is to release my statement. Hopefully, in a week or two, this will all blow over, and we can get back to our lives."

Cassie Meadows had stopped by Dr. Shaw's office to discuss the open Sr. Surgical Nursing position. She had no idea anyone was in his office until she heard voices. She had planned to turn around and come back later, but once she heard Sky's name she quieted and remained outside the door, listening.

*****

Somewhere in the recesses of Sky's sleep clouded mind, she heard her phone buzz. For a few seconds, she ignored it. Instead, she lay nestled inside the warm crook of Remington's arms. Even in twilight, a small smile played around the edges of her lips as she thought about the incredible night they'd had.

Her phone continued to buzz.

*No, not yet.* Sky groaned.

Not that it was possible, but she tried to snuggle even closer to him while breathing in his manly scent. Unfortunately, the bubble they had created for themselves was about to burst. Still, Sky was not ready for the outside world to intrude on their moment, but she had no choice.

*Bzzt Bzzzt! Bzzt Bzzzt! Sky* reached up and answered the phone.

"Dr. Kirby." Her voice was groggy from sleep.

"This is Madison Holly from the Chicago Daily News. I wanted to get a statement from you regarding your involvement in the Charlie Kneeland cover-up."

Sky pushed herself up. "What? What cover-up? Is this a joke?"

"No. We are running a story in our morning paper about your relationship with Kane Langston and his abuse of Charlie Kneeland."

Sky started to choke.

The noise roused Remington from sleep. His eyes opened just a crack until they were fully open. Sky held the silky sheet they slept under crushed to her chest. It may have covered her front, but it didn't do a damn thing to cover her naked body from the back. He stared in admiration at her smooth, caramel-colored skin, thinking about how he had tasted every square inch of it. If by some miracle he had missed a spot, Remington planned to rectify that mistake as soon as she got off the phone.

His hands slid up and down her spine as his fingers caressed her soft skin. Remington had a strong desire to brand Sky as his, and after making love, he felt as if he had done just that.

Remington hadn't been this invested in a woman in years. The feeling was surprising because he didn't think he would ever again. But there was something special about Sky. Remington didn't know if it was because neither of them expected much from the opposite sex or because Charlie's accident had set the stage for them to share their deepest secrets with one another. Remington couldn't call it. He just knew they had been fighting a losing battle of attraction that had been bubbling underneath the surface for too long.

"There has got to be a mistake." Sky's body tensed.

Remington hadn't realized it before because he was caught up in his own thoughts, but something was wrong.

The reporter continued to grill Sky. "So, you deny the cover-up or the relationship?"

"Both! Nothing could be further from the truth. What you are about to print is both slander and defamation. If you do it, I will own the Chicago Daily News!"

"Our sources are pretty solid."

"Then why call me just a few hours away from running the story for a statement?!"

"Due diligence, ma'am."

Sky was going to be sick.

"We received a statement from the Chief-of-Staff, Dr. Shane Shaw. Since it appears as if you are hearing all of this for the first time, I'll read it to you. '*St. Lucia's Hospital is unaware of any rumored relationships between Dr. Sky Kirby and anyone associated with Charlene 'Charlie' Kneeland. However, if there were any signs of abuse the night Ms. Kneeland was admitted, Dr. Kirby was the attending physician. She had a duty—no, a responsibility—to report any suspicions. In her report, there was no mention of abuse. Therefore, based on these new allegations from Bella Lord-*

*Langston, we are launching a full-scale investigation into the matter. And until it is resolved, Dr. Kirby will be placed on administrative leave."*

Sky was speechless.

The reporter continued. "Would you like to change your statement? Did you not report any abuse suspicions due to your rumored romantic relationship with Kane Langston?"

"No comment." Sky disconnected and slowly lowered the phone.

Concerned, Remington sat up and massaged Sky's shoulders. "Everything alright?"

Before she could respond, Remington's own cell started to ring. He whispered into her ear. "I've got to take it. It could be the hospital."

"Wait." Sky placed her hand on his, but Remington had already picked up. His eyes said *I'm sorry.* "Remington."

It was his lawyer. "Rem, where are you?"

He looked at Sky. "I'm not at the hospital."

"I know that. I'm here with Bella. Have you looked at any of your social media accounts?"

"No. I've been asleep."

"Check it, and then high-tail you ass to the hospital. We need to get Charlie moved."

Remington was a little panicked. "Is she okay?"

"She's fine."

"Okay, checking now. I'll call you on the way to the hospital."

Sky mouthed *I need to talk to you.*

Dread crept over him after he disconnected the call and checked his Twitter account.

Sky touched his arm. "It's not true."

After he finished reading, the way Remington looked at Sky sent ice through her veins.

Remington ignored the plea and went to another post. He clicked on the video. Some woman was speaking. "There is a lot to digest folks. Award-winning actress, Bella Lord-Langston, said that she plans to file for a temporary restraining order against and file for divorce from millionaire entrepreneur, Kane Langston. She claims that he was abusive in their relationship and only recently found out that he caused the accident that paralyzed her twelve-year-old daughter, Charlene 'Charlie' Kneeland with billionaire businessman, Remington Kneeland. To make matters worse, there was evidence of the physical abuse, but the attending physician, Dr. Sky Kirby, helped to cover it up because she and Kane were having an affair. There appears to be emails to back up some of these claims."

Remington turned tortured eyes toward Sky. She could see his chest rise and fall. This time it wasn't due to the passion they shared. He was doing his best to control his anger. "I've got to get to Charlie."

Sky saw the affection he had for her drain from his face as she crawled across the bed in an attempt to explain herself. "It's not true. I tried to convince Shane to contact Child Protective Services. He wouldn't, and Noah wouldn't back me up. All I had was my word."

"So, you knew?" Remington wasted no time putting on his clothes. He growled, "I don't give a damn about Child Protective Services." He banged on his chest with his fist. "You should have told me!"

Sky was still trying to plead her case. She stood on her knees in the middle of the bed. "I wanted to. I thought about it a million times. I didn't have any proof, and then I started to doubt myself. Everything else they said was a lie. I'm not having an affair with Kane."

He finished dressing and headed for the door, then turned and penetrated her with a hard stare. "The problem is they were telling the truth about the only thing that I actually care about—Charlie."

Seconds later, Sky jumped at the sound of her front door slamming closed.

*****

Later that morning, Nia walked into Sky's condo. "It's a madhouse out there. I can't separate the paparazzi from the real journalists."

Sky was wearing a bathrobe with her hands wrapped around a hot cup of coffee. "Thanks for coming. This entire thing is crazy. Do you want some?" She lifted up her cup.

Nia hugged her then sat her briefcase down on the sofa next to where Sky took a seat. She pulled out a yellow legal pad. "No. Before we get started, are you okay?"

"I'm feeling so many things all at once, but the dominant emotion is anger."

"Understandable. What the hell happened? Are you really sleeping with Kane? I thought you were sleeping with Remington?"

"Are you asking this as my friend or my lawyer?"

"As your lawyer, I don't give a shit about who you were sleeping with. But as your friend, I need to know what to do to help you get through this. If I don't understand what's really going on, it's going to make helping you difficult."

Sky rolled her neck around her shoulders. "I'm not having an affair with Kane Langston, and until last night, I wasn't sleeping with Remington either."

"Shut up! Finally, you two did the deed. You could see it coming a mile away. The sexual tension was off the charts."

"I'm guessing after today's news, it will be the first and last time. He's pissed at me, and rightfully so."

"I won't lie. It is a lot to swallow. "

"I should have told him that I suspected someone was abusing Charlie."

"So, you did know?" Nia started taking notes.

"I suspected. I wrote it up in my report after the surgery. Protocol for high-level patients is that those types of calls to the police, or any government agency, must be placed by the Chief-of-Staff or his assistant. I fought tooth and nail with Shane and Noah about making the call. Neither of them wanted to stake the reputation of the hospital on my medical opinion."

"Is that what you meant that night when you said he put his career ahead of doing what was right?"

"Yes. They are trying to make me the fall guy. I don't know what happened, but someone had to leak my notes and report to the media about the possible abuse and forged Noah's name on it. Neither Shane nor Noah would have done it. I can see them doing damage control and deciding to blame it all on me. It would kill two birds with one stone."

"There's a special place in hell for people like them. You don't have a copy of the original report do you?"

"No. Not here. At work, but I can't get into the hospital until the suspension is over. My access to everything has been revoked."

Nia nodded. "Okay. I'll subpoena the notes from that night. Alright, tell me everything from the moment you were called in to consult on the case. Don't leave out any detail. By the time I'm done, they'll need to change the name of St. Lucia's Hospital to Sky Kirby Memorial." She took Sky's coffee out of her hand and took a sip. "You might want to make yourself another cup and get comfortable because we've got a lot to cover."

# Chapter 22

Remington arrived at the hospital under a barrage of flashing lights from the media and paparazzi. He barreled his way inside and strode directly over to Charlie. "Are you okay?" He hadn't even noticed Bella standing off to the side.

Charlie's outstretched arms reached for him. "What's happening? What's going on?"

"We're moving you to a new hospital."

"But, why?" She looked genuinely confused.

"Because it's best." Bella spoke. "Where have you been, Remi? It's been a madhouse."

It took everything within him not to strangle her. "No thanks to you and your damned press conference!"

"I finally had the courage to tell the truth, Remi! I know you're upset about the situation, but how do you think I feel. It was my husband she was sleeping with! Not to mention, he did this! He did this to our little girl."

Remington's voice was low and menacing. "You're a piece of work. Sky wasn't sleeping with Kane, and you know it! But even if she were, that's your first concern? Not the so-called abuse? Not Kane causing Charlie's accident? Makes me wonder if any of it is true. I find it hard to believe that Kane abused you. But you both better hope like hell he didn't touch a hair on Charlie's head because if he did, he's a dead man walking."

Remington turned to Charlie to ask if the abuse allegations were true.

Bella cut him off. "It's true! He confessed the entire thing during our last argument. I was afraid for my life. It's why I didn't say anything. But I didn't know about Charlie. It's why I left. I won't allow him to hurt her or me ever again." Bella looked at Charlie to back up her claims. "Isn't that right?"

Charlie's eyes were wide with fear as she looked frantically between her mother and father. She licked her suddenly dry lips. "I-I . . ." Her eyes filled with tears. "I need Sky."

Bella was pissed. She balled her fists upon her hips. "I'm here. Your father's here. What do you need her for?"

"I don't feel so good."

Remington went to her then. He sat down on the bed, accidentally sitting on her leg.

Charlie yelled out. "Ow!"

Remington immediately hopped up. "You felt that?"

"Yes." Tears started streaming down Charlie's face as realization hit her.

At that moment, a medical transport team entered the room. "We are here to prepare Ms. Charlie Kneeland for transport."

# Chapter 23

"This is crazy." Sky rested her head on the back of the sofa. She was exhausted from going over every detail she could remember from the time she received the first phone call from Noah until the day she got the call from the reporter with Nia. They had gone over everything she could think of over the course of several days. "There is nothing else, Nia."

"You better hope there is. Without your notes from that night, this case is ugly."

"But not impossible."

"Only until it's possible. Let's just hope that's before the court date."

That quote was one Sky and Nia used a lot to encourage each other when they were trying to get through medical and law school.

"Have you talked to Remington?" Nia asked.

Sadness fell over Sky's face. "I've left him about a hundred messages. He hasn't responded to any of them."

"It's only been a few days. When he's had enough time to think things through, hopefully, he'll give you an opportunity to explain."

"Explain what exactly? I mean, I think he knows me well enough to know that entire Kane storyline is just that—a lie. But I should have told him about the abuse. I went back and forth over it in my mind a dozen times."

"I thought it was a million?" Nia smiled.

"I wish I could just talk to him. Explain my side. But then I think, really? If Charlie was my daughter, I never would forgive me."

"Forgiveness is weird when you are in love."

"Maybe. But Remington and I aren't in love *love*. I mean, we weren't dating long enough for that, but I think there was something special there."

"There you go being all rational when love is everything but. You can fall in love in a matter of moments."

Sky shook her head. "I don't believe in insta-love."

"Really? So, you can't stop thinking about him? Your heart beats out of your chest when he's around? You would sacrifice anything for him and Charlie? You are not eating or sleeping? So, what exactly would you call that?"

"Stressed the fuck out."

"That might be true, but it doesn't cover how Remington makes you feel."

Realization hit Sky like a ton of bricks. She chewed on her bottom lip. "It's impossible."

"It's only impossible until it's possible. There's no controlling love." Nia thought about her own screwed up love life. "Seems like somebody should invent a pill for that shit. If they could, I would have left Steven by now and given the damn pill to that famous actor, Chris Hemsworth."

As distraught as Sky was she laughed. "I thought you only dated black guys?"

"Unlike you, who has dated a colorful assortment of men, my preference has always been chocolate, but I'd make an exception for him."

"My preference has always been a damn good man. I don't care what color he is, but I have to admit, Remington does it for me."

"Then fight for him! You've been searching for the right man for years. He's the first one I've ever seen you show emotion over. It was weird having you get drunk and cry on my shoulder. The role reversal really had me shook!"

"He's not answering my calls."

"Aren't they at some new rehab facility?"

"Yeah, I haven't been able to find out which one. I think they are using an alias."

"A little birdie told me that they are currently at Serenity Rescue Rehab Center under the name Nala Incredible. Now, aren't you glad we are besties?"

"Are you kidding?"

"Nope, I am so serious."

"Is that a mash-up of characters from the movies The Lion King and The Incredibles?"

Nia giggled. "Yes. And my advice to you is to get in the shower, put something cute on, and head over to that center before they leave. That same birdie told me they will be moving Charlie to a rental at the end of the week. At the rehab center, he can't technically keep you out. Once he moves into the rental, he can keep your ass out by the curb."

*****

Sky was wearing a baseball hat and wearing a dark pair of glasses as she stood outside the Serenity Rescue Rehab center. Her intention was to be incognito just in case the media was lurking somewhere around.

She walked inside with no problem.  Once Sky entered the building, she began to second guess herself but shook off those feelings.  She was willing to do whatever it took to get Remington to forgive her.

As she walked down the hall looking for the room number that Nia's little birdie gave her, Sky stopped short.

Remington was standing in the hallway with his arms folded across his chest listening intently to someone who looked like a physician.  Sky quickly took off her glasses and hat.  She ran her fingers through her hair as she approached them.

The man was speaking.  "Mr. Kneeland, Charlie hasn't been working as hard as I feel she can.  She's making progress, but it's slow."

Remington nodded.  "I'll talk to her."

"I suggest we try to get her to physical therapy tonight to make up for the session she missed earlier today."

Sky knew the moment he noticed her.  Remington's chin lifted slightly as he looked at her over the man's shoulder.  His eyes never left hers as he addressed the man in front of him.  "We'll finish this conversation later."

It must have been the insidiousness of his voice that caused the physician to walk away.  His jaws clenched.  "What are you doing here?"

"Charlie's not going to therapy?"

"Charlie is no longer your concern.  So, again, *why are you here*?"

"Right.  She's not." *But I still care about her.*  Sky swallowed.  "I'm here because you won't answer my calls."

"I'm not answering your calls because I don't want to talk to you." He moved to enter Charlie's room, but Sky touched his arm.

It was as if her touch shot pain through his arm. "Don't."

"I know I messed up but just give me a minute, *please*." Sky pleaded.

Remington didn't answer, but he didn't move either.

Sky new she had about thirty seconds to make her case. She swiped her sweaty palms down the front of her jeans. "I realize that I should have told you about my suspicions. But you know that already. Still, I'm so, so sorry that you feel like I betrayed you. If I could go back in time, I would make a different choice." Sky took a deep breath. "In my wildest dreams, I never would have expected for a twelve-year-old girl and her father to steal my heart. That is what happened. Remington, we connected like I've never connected with another human being. We have something special. We have something real. I made a mistake, but everyone deserves a second chance."

Remington thought about her words.

Nervously, Sky watched him closely. She had laid her feelings bare and could only hope he was willing to give them another try.

"Look," Remington started. "Charlie is my one and only priority right now. She's been put through enough by people who *claim* to care about her. When it comes to her, I don't have the luxury of giving anyone a second chance." He pushed lightly on the door and walked inside closing it behind him.

The loud click was symbolic of so much. Mainly, the crushing of Sky's heart, and the ending of a relationship with the only man she had ever fallen in love with.

# Chapter 24

Omara Johnston-Reid-Hall sat across from her daughter at her favorite restaurant. She whispered. "So, what did you think of Sam? He's great isn't he?"

He actually did seem like a good guy. Maybe her mother had met her prince charming after all. "I like him."

"It's a shame it took an emergency for us to finally meet."

Sky was about to disagree but changed her mind. It was true.

"Don't try to deny it. I'm just glad you called me. It feels good to be needed. Granted, it's been almost two weeks since that fiasco with the hospital, but I don't care why we're meeting. I'm just glad that we are."

"Me too." Sky honestly meant it.

"Do you mean that?"

"I do."

Omara reached across the table and held her hand. "I know how hard it is for you to need people." She chose her words carefully. "Have you talked to them?"

Sky shook her head. "Not since shortly after they left St. Lucia's Hospital. Charlie called a couple of days ago and left a message on my phone, but I haven't called her back. I'm not sure I should." A small smile appeared on Sky's face. "The good news is the feeling in the lower half of her body is getting stronger."

Omara clapped her hands together. "That's fantastic! So, the by-pass surgery you performed was successful."

"Apparently."

"I'm so proud of you. Now, you are one of eleven physicians who has ever performed it successfully. That must be worth at least a congratulations phone call to Charlie, right?"

Sky blew out a breath. "I don't know. She's been through so much. I think her family needs some time to heal." Sky lifted a shoulder. "As far as Remington, I can understand why he doesn't want to talk or have anything to do with me." Sky couldn't help but think it was usually the men who lived down to low expectations, but this time, it was her. "I should have told him my suspicions."

"It sounds like you were caught in-between a rock and a hard place."

She had been, but honesty and trust were a huge part of any relationship. Remington had the same trust issues that Sky had. Not being completely honest with him was a deal breaker and deep down inside, Sky knew it.

"My apologies, ladies. I had to take that call." Her mother's fiancé came back to the table and sat down. "Are you sure you don't want me to pull the trigger with Bella Langston?"

He was a handsome and distinguished looking man with salt and pepper hair. Sky could understand why her mother was attracted to him. Together, they made a striking couple. Omara was just a couple of inches shorter than his six feet. Her mother was not only graceful like a model but had the frame of one too. She wore her hair cut low to her head and tapered around the back and sides. However, Omara would never be caught dead with gray hair. Instead, she wore it natural but colored blonde. It complemented her smooth mocha colored skin.

"Thank you, Sam, for being willing to use your position and influence as the President of the Creative Artistry Agency on my behalf. But I've had some time to think about it, and regardless of how I feel about her mother's wicked ways, Charlie still loves her, and I love Charlie. I know, someday, Bella will get hers."

Sam placed his hands on top of Sky's mother's in a loving gesture. "Well, if you change your mind, let me know. In the meantime, let's talk about something positive. Your mother and I have set a date for the wedding. We figured Monaco next month."

Sky choked on the water she was sipping. "Already? You two have only been dating for a few months. I thought you were going to have a long engagement."

"When you know you know." Sam continued to look at her mother lovingly.

Before Sky met Remington, she would never have understood that sentiment. Now that she had the experience of being with him, and being briefly touched by love, she understood it completely. "Just let me know the day and time. I'll be there."

Omara was shocked. "My god. It happened." Sky's mother's eyes grew glassy.

"What?" Sky looked on curiously.

"You know what being in love feels like." Omara placed her hand over her heart.

Exaggerating the move, Sky checked the watch on her arm. "Would you look at the time. I've got to meet Nia. We're negotiating my settlement."

Omara would let her off the hook for now, but they were going to talk about it. "That's right. But delayed is not denied. We will talk. Call me when it's over, and we'll discuss *everything*."

Sky stood and kissed her mother on the cheek. "I will. Love you." She turned to Sam. "It was a pleasure meeting you."

Sam had stood when Sky had. "It was a pleasure meeting you as well."

As they watched Sky walk away, Omara wiped a tear from her eye. She twisted her body toward her new fiancé. "I've just witnessed a miracle. Love can change anyone."

*****

Sky was having a final meeting with Nia before they met with the hospital's legal team.

"I'm going to start charging you extra for house calls." Nia pulled her knees up on Sky's sofa as she took a bite of her chicken salad.

"Mmhmm . . . then I'm going to start charging you for groceries."

"Oooohhh . . . you're extra cranky today. I take it the lunch with your mother didn't go well."

"Actually, it went very well."

Nia raised her eyebrows. "I still can't believe you called Omara Johnston-Reid-Hall to help you cripple Bella. Before we get into that, what did you think of her fiancé? Is he going to help you?"

Sky's tone was determined. "I had planned to hit Bella so hard that it would drop her to her knees."

They were interrupted when the buzzer to Sky's door sounded.

She hadn't been able to get out of her funk since the moment the reporter called and ruined her life. "If someone from the paparazzi has snuck into this building again . . ."

Nia responded. "The restraining order I filed should take care of that, so whoever it is I hope it's not them." She hopped up off the sofa and blocked Sky's path. "I'll get it. Now that I think about it, if it is someone from the media, I don't need you going to the door giving them a money shot and blowing my case."

Nia padded barefoot over to the door and opened it. "Dr. Kirby isn't taking any questions from the press today except to say *NO COMMENT*!"

"Oh. I'm not with the media. My name is Cassandra Meadows. I'm a nurse at St. Lucia's, and I have some information that I think might be helpful to her case."

More than a little interested, Nia stepped aside and allowed Cassie to come in. Sky was standing just a few feet away with her hands folded across her chest. "Cassandra? What are you doing here?"

"I wanted to give you this." It was a thick manila envelope.

"What's in it?"

"My notes from Charlie Kneeland's surgery along with everything you sent me."

Sky stared at the folder with new eyes as if it were the Holy Grail. "You're kidding?"

"No. I am not. I would have been here sooner, but I recently moved and had to find it in all of my boxes. I couldn't print off the copy you sent me at work because the hospital wiped any digital files associated with you."

Nia frowned. "Thanks for that bit of information. That's *ILLEGAL*. I guess I'll add destroying evidence to my long list of grievances. My forensic IT specialist would eventually find them, but that's if we have to go to court, and that could take forever, our arbitration meeting with the hospital is tomorrow."

Cassie smiled. "Too bad for them that I had already printed it, made a copy to review, and taken it home."

Nia asked, "What exactly is in the folder?"

Sky was breathless. *"Everything.* It's the original report that I sent to Cassie. It should have a date and time stamp on the printouts." Sky emptied the contents of the envelope. "The procedure was a complex one. And since St. Lucia's is a teaching hospital, there should have been . . ." Her voice trailed off.

Cassie finished the sentence for her. "Video."

A flash drive slid out of the envelope. Sky closed her eyes and pressed the little piece of metal to her chest.

"That's not all, Dr. Kirby. I also wrote down notes from the discussion you and Dr. Bridges had. I figured if I were ever in the same situation, I would know how to proceed. You very clearly felt that the bruises on her posterior dorsal, the thorax, and the upper right quadrant of her abdomen were not the product of the fall. I heard you clearly state, the bruises looked several days old and that you thought someone might have 'beat the hell out of her.' Dr. Bridges disagreed. He said you didn't have facts to support your claim and that if you wrote it down in your report, he wasn't going to back you up."

"You heard him say that?" Nia asked.

Cassie nodded.  "Yes, I did, and it's on the video.  The recording equipment was still on in the O.R., and I was standing in the doorway.  It's distant, but you can hear their conversation."

"Would you be willing to make an official statement, maybe even testify if necessary?"

Cassie nodded again.  "I also think I know who leaked the reports that made it look like Dr. Kirby was covering up Charlie Kneeland's abuse to the press."

"Who?" Nia and Sky asked at the same time.

"Jazlyn."

"Why would she do that?"  Nia asked.

"Well, she kinda has a thing for Dr. Bridges."

Sky couldn't believe it.  Then again, she could.  Jazlyn was a loose end she should have tied up.  "We're not together anymore."

"Regardless, he's still preoccupied with you.  Jazlyn had been talking about you a lot to the other nurses, asking us questions, especially about Charlie Kneeland's surgery.  I didn't think anything of it until all this came out . . . then it clicked. It had to be her. I mean, just giving the press enough information to make *you* look bad would be enough for her, getting you fired would be a bonus.  Chief-of-Staff Shaw and Dr. Bridges think the same thing. I overheard a conversation they had, saying as much . . . AND how they were going to cover it up and blame it on you." Nia's ears perked up at Cassie's last comment. Before she could say anything, Cassie added, "I'll testify to overhearing that too. I couldn't just stand by and let them ruin your career and reputation, Dr. Kirby." Cassie paused. "Anyway, I've got to get back to the hospital. I just hope these documents are helpful."

"You've been more than helpful. If what Sky has in her hands proves to be what you say it is, I'll bury those assholes in court and sue Bella Langston for defamation." Nia was ready for war, and now, she was armed for it.

Sky stopped Cassie before she walked out the door. "Thank you." Sky's voice was full of sincere emotion.

Cassie beamed. "You're more than welcome, Dr. Kirby."

After Sky closed the door, she turned back to Nia.

"So where does Bella's part come into all this? Do you think she and Jazlyn were working together? Why would she do that?" Words were coming out of Nia's mouth, but she was concentrating on the papers from the envelope.

"No." Sky shook her head. "No, she was pissed at me. She thought I was sleeping with Remington and had come to my office to threaten me. I think it was just an opportunity that presented itself at the right time. She probably got a call from the press, and when she found out what they knew, she jumped on it. She's an actress. It's not hard to believe that she'd make that all up on a whim.  She puts on quite a performance at the hospital all the time."

"If that's true, I wonder what Kane did to her.  Why would she say the two of you were having an affair?" Nia asked, not looking up from the papers.

"Maybe she was just trying to take the suspicion off herself. Or maybe she was pissed at him too.  I don't know.  Time will tell." Sky sighed.

"Well, whatever the reason.  I'm going to bury her . . . all of them. This . . ." Nia held up the papers, ". . . this changes everything."

"I'm all for burying Shane and Noah but not Bella.  I don't want to hurt Charlie any more than this fiasco already has.  Not publicly anyway. That's what I was trying to tell you earlier, but Bella doesn't have to know that.  Scare the shit out of her.  Threaten that if she doesn't make a public apology and retract her statements about me that I will sue her for defamation and every dime she has."

# Chapter 25

Bella had been flirting with Remington ever since they moved Charlie to the new facility.

He could barely stand to be in the same room with her and, based on Charlie's interactions with her, he didn't think she could either. Remington was no longer sure that Bella being MIA was such a bad thing.

His mood didn't have a chance to improve since he couldn't keep his mind off Sky. Today, though, Remington was going to be happy even if it killed him. Charlie was going home. She was being discharged. It had been a long road, and she still had a mountain to climb, but she was moving in the right direction. If nothing else, Remington had to be thankful to Sky for that.

The room was quiet as the three of them waited for the medical transport team to arrive when Kane burst into Charlie's room. "You lying bitch!"

Shocked, Bella's eyes went wide. "What are you doing here!?"

"I knew this would be the best place to find you since you've been hiding behind your gates. It's bad enough that you've sicced your PR team on me and brought me up on bogus charges, but now my bank accounts are frozen! All this because I want a divorce!?" He growled out.

It only took two steps for Remington to grab him by his shirt and for his fist to go crashing into his nose. He heard it crunch.

Kane tried to fight back, but he didn't have a chance. Remington landed another hard blow. "I should kill you for what you did to my daughter. You're the reason she's in here!" Remington slammed his fist into Kane's stomach, causing him to double over.

"No, I'm not! I can prove it!"

Bella screamed. "You're disgusting, Kane! You know what you did."

"No, I know what you did!" He spat back.

Remington landed another punch to the side of Kane's head that looked as if it had knocked him out. Blood gushed from his nose and mouth.

"Daddy, no! Please. You're going to kill him!" Charlie screamed. "It wasn't him. Kane didn't cause me to fall off the horse. There was no horse!"

Kane choked on his words. "Ask Bella why she paid the security guard to move Charlie's body after the accident."

"You piece of shit!" Remington spat the words at Kane before turning to Charlie. "I know he caused your bruises." His voice almost broke. "I know he was abusing you! You almost died because of him." A fresh round of rage went through Remington, only this time the security from the center burst through the doors and held him back.

Charlie was crying almost hysterically. "Yes, he had caused the bruises a few days before, but I didn't fall off a horse! Mom pushed me out of the window."

The room went silent.

Kane nodded. "I just found out today when that same security guard left a message on my cell phone, thinking it was Bella's. Our numbers are very similar . . . one digit off. He said she paid him to move Charlie's body from below her bedroom window next to the stable.  She paid him off for his silence and his help. I believed her lies too!"

Bella couldn't believe Charlie didn't stick to the plan.  "W-what? That's not true.  That's a lie!"

"It is true!"  Charlie's eyes pleaded with her father.  "You have to believe me.  I was going to run away because I got kicked out of school. Mommy caught me planning to leave.  She started hitting me and saying I was the reason she and Kane were having so many problems.  I tried to get away, and I kept walking backward toward my bedroom window.  It was open, and she pushed too hard.  I fell out of it.  The next thing I knew I woke up in the hospital."  Charlie turned sad eyes at Bella.  "I'm sorry, Mom."

Bella looked nervously around the room.  "The injury to your head must have been worse than we thought for you to come up with a crazy story like that."

Charlie was doubled over as she wailed gut-wrenching sobs.

Remington was sick to his stomach.  He couldn't even look at Bella. "Get her out of here before I'm the one being hauled out in handcuffs."

"Remi, this is madness!  I would never!"  Bella tried to explain.  All of her hard work to win Charlie and Remington back was disintegrating right before her eyes.

Remington had a murderous rage pumping through his veins. He roared, "Get out!  Get. The. Fuck. Out. Before I really lose it.  And while you're at it, call a good lawyer because I will be pressing charges."

Serenity security grabbed Bella and Kane. She struggled against them. "It was an accident! Do you really think I would hurt Charlie on purpose?"

They were dragged out before Remington completely lost total control.

*****

Sky and Nia were walking down the hallway toward the hospital's executive conference room. Nia continued to coach Sky, telling and retelling her the game plan. "They are going to try to *BS* us. Don't get rattled or angry enough to lash out. We have their balls in a vice-grip. By-the-way, I broke up with Steven last night—for good this time."

Sky almost tripped over her Louboutin. "You didn't?"

"I did. Honestly, I saw how happy Remington made you. I mean, I know your relationship is kind of a mess, but I have a feeling with some time, you'll find your way to each other. Anyway, it's been nothing but hell with Steven for years. I won't be able to find the man that will give me the kind of natural high you had with Remington if I'm afraid to let Steven go for fear of being alone. So, I ended it." They stood in front of the conference door. "We'll toast to a new beginning later. In the meantime, are you ready?"

Sky couldn't wait for later. She pulled Nia into a quick hug. "I'm armed with the best lawyer in Chicago. Of course, I'm ready."

They opened the door to find several members of the Board of Directors and their lawyers sitting around the conference table. The men all stood when they entered. Nia nodded. "Good afternoon, gentlemen." Of course, it wasn't surprising that she and Sky would be the only women in the room.

They took their seats. Nia at the head of the table, and Sky kitty-corner to her.

Nia was no-nonsense. "Let's make this as painless as possible and get to business. My client has suffered irreparable harm at the hands of this institution. We won't accept anything less than a full public apology from the hospital, Dr. Kirby being reinstated to her former position, and that the Chief-of-Staff, Dr. Shane Shaw, along with his assistant, Dr. Noah Bridges must resign immediately. Also, Jazlyn Farrow must be *fired* for leaking private medical information to the press."

"Is that all?"

"No. I failed to mention that we'll need St. Lucia's to throw in a nice check for five-million dollars deposited into Dr. Kirby's personal account for all the hardships this ordeal has caused."

The lead attorney for the hospital looked at the Chief-Financial-Officer for his approval. He nodded in agreement. "Done."

Nia was shocked. It was much too easy. She was going to push the envelope. "And another five million to be donated to a Spinal Cord Injury research organization of my clients choosing."

Another nod.

"Agreed." The lead attorney didn't allow Nia another moment to ask for something else. "If that's all, draw up the necessary paperwork and send it over to my office. Hopefully, we can get this all resolved by five p.m."

Nia was on the verge of another ask when Sky tapped her with her foot under the table and gave her a slight head shake. She shot Sky a glare that only she would recognize. Instead of being greedy, Nia clapped her hands together and followed her client's lead. "Yes, I'll have my office do that."

"Great, then I think we're done." Everyone stood. The meeting couldn't have last any longer than fifteen minutes. Some of the members left as Nia began to pack up her things.

Just as the lead attorney was about to leave, she stopped him. "I'm sorry, your name is Jude Lawrence, right?"

"Yes. It's on my card." Before he handed it to her, he scribbled something on the back. "My personal number if you need it for some reason."

Nia smiled then got back on her lawyerly game. "What happened? It took us longer to prepare for this meeting than the meeting itself."

He looked around Nia to Sky. "Let's just say someone with deep pockets decided to take matters into their own hands and make this easy for everyone." He sent a sexy smile toward Nia. "If you want more details, call me. We can meet over drinks and discuss it." He tilted his chin toward Nia then Sky and walked out of the door leaving them alone to ponder his words.

The room was almost empty except for them until a very familiar voice joined theirs.

"Ms. Nia Lexington, do you think I could have a private word with Dr. Kirby?"

Nia looked up to see a man too gorgeous for words. Remington was much better looking in person. He wore a custom-tailored chocolate suit that complemented his tanned skin and would make an Armani model jealous. When he walked past, his cologne made Nia's insides clench. She was almost tongue-tied. "Um . . . Yes. Of course. Sky, I'll meet you downstairs in say fifteen minutes." Nia winked at her then left and closed the door.

Remington stood with his back to Sky and hands in his front pockets, staring out the window.

Sky was more than surprised to see Remington. Shocked was a better word. She blurted out the first thing that came to mind. "How is Charlie?"

"She's getting better."

"Then why are you here? Is she here? Does she need tests?" Sky was concerned. Although she had made a mistake by omitting her concerns to Remington, she wasn't going to let him get away with disrespecting her. "Look, you wanted to have a conversation, so can you at least turnaround. I'm not going to talk to your back."

Slowly, Remington did as she asked. "No. Charlie is not here. We've rented a house in Chicago for a while. She asked that I come to this meeting because she wanted me to make sure that you were okay." Seeing Sky in person was harder than he thought it would be. She still took his breath away. In truth, he wanted to make sure she was okay too.

Sky whispered. "Incredible that after everything that has happened she's thinking of me. Can you tell Charlie that I miss her too? Please tell her that I think of her often and that I'm sorry I didn't call her back." Sky blew out a long breath. *Speaking of I'm sorries. I hate that I ruined whatever possibility there was between us,* she thought. Sky didn't plan on apologizing again. She had been sincere and had done it enough. Once more wasn't going to make Remington finally see the light and forgive her.

His voice was pained. "I trusted you."

It hurt her to know that she hurt him. "I know. And I'm sure it doesn't matter, but I wanted to tell you. At the time, I honestly didn't know what the right thing to do was."

Remington couldn't find words.

Sky waited, but when he didn't say anything, she started to gather her things. "I should go."

"Wait." Remington walked slowly over to her. He was standing only inches away. "I'm not only here on behalf of Charlie, but I'm also here because I had some unfinished business, and I *needed* to see you."

Sky searched his eyes for answers. "Why?"

Remington ran his hands through his hair. "As angry as I am, I can't stop thinking about us. I can't stop thinking about and wanting you."

Sky couldn't believe what she was hearing. "What? Is this some kind of cruel joke?"

"I would never joke about what's in my heart."

She erased the distance between them and stood on her tiptoes as she continued to look Remington in his eyes. Sky could only hope he could see the truth in hers. "I've never felt for anyone the way that I feel about you."

He placed her hand over his heart. "You feel that?" It pumped hard and fast. "Just being near you throws it out of control and makes it hard to breathe. It's a scary feeling. Even after everything, you're worth it, and what we found is real. I can't let my hang-ups from my past dictate my future and cause me to miss out on something great."

"Do you really mean that?"

"Yeah, I do—"

Before he could finish his sentence, Sky kissed him lightly on the lips.

Remington leaned in and deepened it as he pulled her into a tight embrace. After a moment, he broke the kiss.

Sky was basking in the euphoria of it, especially after dreaming about kissing him for so many nights, she didn't want it to end. Her eyes were still closed when she spoke. "The hospital is going to make things right with everything that happened here. I hope we can put this all behind us and move on."

"I know, and we will as long as we want to. I for one am ready to move on . . . with you." Remington touched his forehead to hers.

Her eyes fluttered open and stared at him questioningly. "How did you know the hospital is going to make it right? Nia just negotiated the deal not ten minutes ago."

Remington gave her his trade-mark lop-sided grin that made her knees go weak. "I wasn't about to let this hospital destroy your career, so I bought it to make sure."

"Are you kidding?" He couldn't have been serious. "You bought the hospital?"

"I know how important your career and reputation is. No matter how angry I was, I knew you wouldn't sleep with Kane. I knew you would never be behind a cover-up. I just hated you didn't tell me the truth. We have to be honest with each other no matter how hard it is."

Sky's eyes started to water. "Okay."

"At the end of the day, you saved my daughter's life. And since I'm falling in love with you, buying the hospital was the least I could do. There would be no chance of starting over if your career was in tatters."

Sky could barely form words. *Did he just say he thought he was falling in love with me?* "I'm falling in love with you too."

Remington grinned. "That is good to hear since someone told me 'Don't mess this up.' So, in my effort not to do just that, would you like to have dinner with Charlie and me tonight?"

Sky's unshed tears spilled over. "There is no place I would rather be."

# Epilogue

*One year later*

Remington was decked out in a black tuxedo and tie as he paced back and forth in the foyer. He was nervous. "C'mon, Charlie, she's going to be here any minute."

"I'm coming, Dad." Slowly, Charlie rounded the corner in the new ranch-style mansion that her father had built specifically with her disability in mind. It boasted of wider than normal hallways and was equipped with ramps and more. Tonight the home sparkled with a different kind of energy that had nothing to do with the large chandelier that hung above them.

Charlie was dressed in a beautiful tea-length yellow gown. It brought out her silky golden curls that had been pulled back into a messy ponytail as she walked on her own two feet with just the assistance of a walker. "Is she here yet?"

Remington checked his watch. "Not yet, but she should be any minute. Wow. You look beautiful."

Charlie blushed. "Thanks. Special night, special dress."

Sophia and Yolanda came out of the shadows. "Is she here?"

"Not yet," Remington answered.

"Well, everything is all set, Mr. Remington. The wine is chilling, and everything you've asked for is in place."

"Thank you, Sophia."

The doorbell rang.

"It's her." Charlie and Yolanda said in unison.

Remington took a deep breath and opened the door.

Sky stood on the other side. She wore a form-fitting, candy-apple red dress with a plunging neckline that hugged all her generous curves. She didn't wear any accessories. She didn't need them, not when her full, kissable bow-shaped lips were covered in a bold red lipstick. The color complemented her smooth caramel skin. Remington's eyes smoldered as he visualized, not just taking off the dress and lipstick, but *how* he planned to do it. Considering his daughter, her best friend and mother were standing right behind him, he needed to tamp down his illicit thoughts.

The heat in his eyes made Sky's stomach flutter. Even after dating for over a year, Remington still made her heart race. As she stepped over the threshold, Sky was unable to look away from his gaze. Remington had a way of shrinking the size of a room. He could make her feel like nothing existed outside the two of them.

"Wow. You look amazing, Sky," Charlie said in awe.

Her voice brought them back from whatever world they had absconded to.

"I second that. You look beautiful." Remington leaned over and placed a lingering kiss on Sky's cheek, whispering into her ear, "I know you look even better underneath that dress, and I can't wait to see."

His words put a saucy smile on her face. Sky's response was for his ears only as she pulled back and gazed into those gray eyes. "Maybe we should skip the fundraiser and find out."

"Hmm . . . Don't tempt me."

Sky looked around Remington to see several pairs of eyes staring at them. She cleared her throat and moved out of his embrace. "Thank you, everyone, for the compliments, but we all know the bell of the ball is Charlie Kneeland. You look fantastic! Is that the lip-gloss we bought the other day?"

"Yep. It sure is."

Remington wasn't about to get caught up in a bout of girl talk. He stopped it before they got started. "Before we leave, I have something I want to show you. Can you follow me into the study?"

"Aren't we going to be late?"

"We've got a little time."

Sky placed her hand in his and followed behind. As they entered Remington's private study, her mouth dropped into a perfectly shaped *O*. "Remington? What have you done?" Breathlessly, Sky turned around in a circle.

"I had it decorated based on what Charlie and I could glean from you. Do you like it? I figured this could be your office."

Sky smirked and placed a hand on her hip. "Then why do you have a desk in here too?"

He lifted a shoulder. "Sometimes, I just don't want to be away from you. If it were up to me you would never leave this house, but you and your rules."

"My mother has been engaged six times. I've learned a thing or two from that. Her motto to me was always, *'don't be a wife until you are a wife.'* This is your home, and that's fine."

Remington chuckled. "Funny, I don't remember you saying that to the architect."

Sky looked sheepish. "I just wanted to make sure you and Charlie were comfortable."

"Right. Of course."

Sky turned her back to him as she continued to admire, not only how Remington furnished and decorated the room, but also the lovely white roses placed all around. "No one has ever done anything this sweet for me." It was a big gesture for a man who said he had never wanted to get married again or have any more children. For a moment, Sky's heart was heavy because she wanted those things with Remington.

She sighed, wistfully.

Sky didn't know what the future held, but she was willing to take the journey wherever it led. "We should probably get moving, or we are really going to be late."

When Sky turned to face Remington, he was on bended knee, holding a little black velvet box.

Her breath caught, and her hands went to her throat. "Oh, my god! What are you doing?"

"I *thought* you were special the moment we met. I *knew* it after experiencing the tender loving care you showed Charlie and me during one of the most difficult times in our lives. I've been lucky to have an opportunity to get to really know you, and the time we have spent together has only confirmed that you are more incredible than I already thought. It drives me insane that I don't get to wake up to you every morning and fall asleep with you every night. I plan to change that because . . ." Remington paused. "I love you and want to spend the rest of my life with you. I hope you feel the same. If so, then Sky Kirby Johnston will you marry me?"

Tears filled her eyes.

Remington opened the black box and inside was a flawless seven-carat, emerald cut yellow diamond. He took it out and held it up to Sky, ready to place it on her finger.

His hands shook slightly. "Sky?"

"Yes?"

"Is that yes you'll marry me, or yes that you hear me?"

"Both! Yes! Yes, yes, YES!"

He placed the ring on her finger.

Sky threw her arms around his neck and kissed him.

The door burst open, and not only did Charlie, Sophia, and Yolanda enter the room but so did Sky's mother and husband number four, Sam, Nia and her new boyfriend, Sky's father, Franklin, and Remington's dad, Michael Kneeland.

Sophia brought celebratory champagne into the room and sparkling apple juice for the girls so that they could join in on the toast.

Sky's mother was the first to pull Sky into a tight embrace. She couldn't contain her excitement as she pulled her away. "I knew there was something special about Remington. Congratulations, honey!"

Charlie stood at Omara's elbow, waiting for her turn to congratulate Sky and her dad. She held a bouquet of yellow roses, and when it was her turn, she handed them to Sky. "Here. These are for you. They are not from Dad. They are from me." Her eyes were glassy.

"Thank you. They are beautiful." Sky's throat was thick. "Are you okay with this?"

The room quieted as everyone watched.

"Are you kidding me? I'm better than okay. I'm ecstatic! I even helped Daddy plan the proposal." Her voice turned a little somber. "With my real mom thousands of miles away, I would love to have you here full-time." Charlie wrapped her arms around Sky's waist, and Sky returned the hug with equal fervor.

The happy tears Sky had been battling back, slid down her cheek. "I know I'm not your mom, and I'd never try to replace her, but I hope you know that I've fallen in love with you just as much as I have your father. You could even say, if it weren't for you, we might have never found one another." Sky's smile grew so big it spread across her entire face.

Remington didn't want to spend one second thinking about Bella and Kane. He was happy that Bella had moved away and was shamefully doing a bit part on an unpopular soap opera. The Great Bella Lord-Langston had fallen far from grace. However, he had heard through Charlie that she was engaged to some millionaire hedge fund manager. Remington had had him checked out only to find that, unbeknownst to Bella, the man was millions of dollars in debt. It served her right. She had better be glad that Charlie pleaded on her behalf. It was the only thing that had kept Bella's ass out of prison. That and signing over full legal and physical custody. Kane, on the other hand, Remington didn't give a shit about. Charges had been brought up against him for abusing Charlie, but Kane turned on Bella and it became a game of he said, she said. For Charlie's sake, Remington had the charges dropped. However, a few tips were provided to the authorities, and Kane was currently serving one year of a five-year Federal prison term for tax-evasion. It wasn't what he really deserved, but at least it was something.

There was no doubt in Remington's mind that over the past year he had made the right decisions. For the first time in a long time, he was looking forward to a future. A future that included, at least, two more children. He smiled inwardly thinking about how Sky had made sure his home had enough room for at least that many. His smile turned into a full-on grin thinking about it as he shook hands with Sky's father and step-father.

Remington's own father waited patiently to get his son's full attention. When it was his turn, the older Mr. Kneeland pulled him into a bear hug. His voice was full of emotion. "Last week, when you brought Sky to meet your mom, I still can't believe she found her way back to us for just long enough to thank Sky for putting the twinkle back into your eyes. If I ever had any doubts, at that moment, they were squashed. I hope you thanked her for giving me just another few minutes with the love of my life."

Remington wasn't sure he could speak after his father's comment.

Just a few feet away, Sky saw the emotion from the conversation with his father all over Remington's face.

She made her way through the well-wishers to him and grabbed hold of Remington's hand as she kissed her soon-to-be father-in-law on the cheek. Remington felt the comforting pressure. Sky was the balm to his soul. It gave him the moment he needed to collect himself.

Remington pulled Sky into the crook of his arm and looked around to see all the people in the room. *This* was living. Surrounded by the people he loved the most and ready to start a new.

Remington had often wondered what would happen when an immovable object met an unstoppable force . . . He now knew the answer.

They fell in love.

# Thank You

I hope you enjoyed Remington's Sky.  If so, Please leave a review.

**Join Author LaShawn Vasser's newsletter for Advanced Reader Copies, Giveaways, and Information regarding upcoming releases.**
PLEASE JOIN HERE.

# Other Books by LaShawn Vasser

## MAGNETIC ATTRACTION (THE HOT VOLTAGE SERIES BOOK 2)

*Where was Austin McKenzie? Was he dead or alive?*

Everyone wanted to know, and Bo Stratton was determined to find out. But what would it cost her?

Austin was last seen protecting the people he loved from a serious threat, but when that threat was gone . . . so was he.

Falling in love while the world suffered a cataclysmic attack the likes of an apocalypse wasn't really the best timing, but for Austin and Bo, their passion could not be denied. Bo's false sense of safety exploded in dramatic fashion—only to be overshadowed by the loss of Austin. As more threats appear, she's not sure what's more dangerous; her new reality or the appearance of Logan Miles.

The sexy Logan Miles was rugged, handsome, and had an irresistible charm. He also helped to save the lives of Bo's family. For his reward, Logan wanted *her*. There was just one problem—Bo's heart belonged to Austin McKenzie. *But would it always*? Can Bo fight the magnetic attraction that seems to be building between them?

Find out that and more in Magnetic Attraction, Book 2 in the Hot Voltage Series.

## MAGNETIC PULSE (THE HOT VOLTAGE SERIES BOOK 1)

It wasn't a chance encounter or love at first sight that brought Bo Stratton and Austin McKenzie together, but fear, desperation, and need. That trio of emotions kept them close. Close enough for Bo to realize that Austin makes her heart race . . . her blood boil . . . and her body pulse. Unfortunately, she can't stand him. As a matter of fact, she would like to be as far away from him as possible. There was just one small problem . . . calamity has forced them together.

Maybe there wasn't just one problem - *her dislike for Austin McKenzie could only be rivaled by her attraction.*

Magnetic Pulse is book one in the Hot Voltage Series. Follow the events that lead Bo and Austin on an unbelievable journey as society begins to unravel and they fall in love.

## PIECES OF ME (A CONTEMPORARY BROKEN HEARTS ROMANCE – Book 1)

Davis Chatham is a ruthless billionaire who spends every waking moment building Chatham Industries. That is until he meets and marries the woman of his dreams, Anne Mathews. However, his workaholic lifestyle destroys their marriage. After trying and failing to win her back Davis was left divorced, broken and bitter. Nothing he tried could soothe his restless soul until he met Nicole DonLeavy on that fateful night of the plane crash.

Get to know Davis Chatham and Nicole DonLeavy as they struggle to survive on an island paradise and follow what unfolds when Anne comes back into his life after their rescue. Is it possible to be in love with two women? And faced with a choice, which one will he choose? This is not your typical love story.

## FRAGMENTS OF US (A CONTEMPORARY BROKEN HEARTS ROMANCE – Book 2)

Who has the perfect love story? Certainly not Mr. and Mrs. Chatham . . .

It's been five years since Davis and Nicole said their *I. Dos—five years, two children, and a mansion on the hill, let's not forget . . . their very own island.* Perfect love story right? *Wrong.* Not when old habits die hard, and new ones are worse than the old.

This will be the ultimate fight for survival and takes them back to where it all started. In *Fragments of Us*, Davis and Nicole can only hope to put the broken pieces of their lives back together.

## THE ROOM (A SENSUOUS EXPERIENCE)

Robyn Levy was over chasing the superficial. Her days were empty and downright unsatisfying.

Wake up.

Work hard.

Spend her nights alone.

And, start all over again . . . until she entered **THE ROOM**.

Maxwell Bryant has always known exactly what he wanted and stopped at nothing to get it.
But one goal continued to remain elusive. Or, was it finally within reach?

Find out what happens in **THE ROOM – A Sensuous Experience**.

## A RESERVATION FOR ONE (The Untamed Love Series Book 1)

Haven Shaw wouldn't consider her love life a tragedy romance just . . . tragic. A disaster. A catastrophe. She wanted off the break-up and make-up crazy train that left her unable to recognize herself.

Her plan. End the ridiculousness and focus on getting control of her life.

His plan. Which one?

Love's plan. Amp up the crazy.

Love and life were about to get much more complicated.

## A RESERVATION FOR TWO (The Untamed Love Series Book 2)

Haven Shaw learned the hard way that even after messy break-ups, broken hearts, and the loss of loved ones . . . life goes on.

She was fully prepared to meet the challenges of her future alone. That was her plan.

Too bad her plan, his plan, and love's plan were never on the same page.

Find out how it all unfolds in part 2 of the Untamed Love Series - A Reservation for Two

## FEVERISH UNBROKEN

Imani Jones Hadley thought she'd made the best decision of her life by marrying Garrett Tristan Hadley. The second she laid eyes on him, he made her body tingle and her toes curl.

Yes, he came with baggage. Didn't they all? Only she didn't know it was the kind that would have her losing her mind! Less than two years later, Imani wanted out. She wanted a divorce STAT.

Too bad Garrett had different ideas. Despite their impossible situation, Imani left him feverish—a kind of feverish unbroken.

He was never going to let her go.


## THE ONE THAT SLIPPED AWAY

Harrison Haughton messed up. He made the biggest mistake of his life and knew it the moment Mia Jamison left him.

Every attempt to win her back has failed except for one. The letter. His last hope, the one Harrison poured his heart into, but even it eventually came back—Returned to Sender. Only then did he accept the truth. It was over. A part of him knew that this was the kind of loss he'd carry for a lifetime.

It took Mia Jamison years to recover from a broken heart only to meet the perfect man - a good man, a strong man with ambitions, and one who checked all the boxes on her list. If only . . .

If only, coming face-to-face with Harrison Haughton didn't open up Pandora's Box.

No more hiding. It was time deal with a past that had the potential to destroy more than one future.

## A STORM IS COMING (The Storm Series Book 1)

THIS IS BOOK ONE OF TWO

A Storm Is Coming is about a beautiful and tough as nails corporate attorney, Braylee Hinsdale, who must use every trick in the book to keep the handsome and powerful Alexandro Manchetti from losing everything.

Alexandro is powerful, handsome, ridiculously sexy and has just suffered an unimaginable loss. He needs her skills as a ruthless attorney to win a case that he's being told is unwinnable. It is unlike anything Braylee has ever faced and will demand everything from her.

Some have said they can sense when A Storm Is Coming, but neither were prepared for the storms ahead.

## A PERFECT STORM (The Storm Series Book 2)
THIS IS BOOK TWO OF TWO - CAN BE READ AS A STANDALONE.

A death and the potential loss of Manchetti Enterprises brought powerhouse attorney, Braylee Hinsdale together with Alexandro Manchetti. She managed the impossible - saved his business and his sanity. In turn, he was able to pierce through her tough armor and gently remove an intractable mask concealing deeply hidden wounds. While their attraction was immediate, each fought to protect their fragile hearts from hurt and harm; but instead found strength and love.

Just as Alexandro and Braylee seemed on the path to happily ever after, they found themselves in the middle of a storm. A powerful storm. A Perfect Storm. And it had the name Gina Lee Xiou written all over it. Who was she? A lover from his past? What did she want? More importantly, could she blow up their lives with just a few words? And would she dare? Find out in A Perfect Storm.

## THE RIGHT SIDE OF MY PILLOW
Cricket Anderson and Cole Thornton were throwaways. The outside world didn't have room for them. Yet, from the tender age of nine, all they had was each other...until they didn't. Not only were promises broken but so was Cricket's heart.

Focused and driven to create a life made of dreams, Cole Thornton succeeded only to be left feeling empty and alone. Ten years later, a chance encounter brings him together with the one person he's ever felt connected to—an angry, disconnected and broken woman.

They say time heals all wounds. But can two damaged souls

discover love and mend their hollowed hearts? Find out in The Right Side of My Pillow.

## CREE

Cree Jacobs has ever only loved one man, and for years she's worked two jobs, sometimes three to support his dreams. Her entire world centered around Cameron Jacobs. What happens when his world no longer revolves around her?

Distance has kept them apart for so long that they've become virtual strangers. Feeling lost and alone Cree realized his goals were her goals. His dreams were her dreams until tragic events forced a path of self-discovery.

Sometimes you have to stop, regroup, and find your center. Will that center lead back to love?

## The Stranger Next To Me

Tasha Stevens and Sabrina Links-Horne have been best friends since high school. Everyone always wondered how their friendship stood the test of time. Especially since they were polar opposites in every way, except for one thing. They were both in love with Tim Horne . . . Sabrina's husband.

Although they've seen each other through the best and worst of times, one decision will change the course of their lives forever and leave them both wondering who is The Stranger Next to Me?

## Out of Nowhere (Out of Nowhere Series)

THIS IS BOOK ONE OF THREE

He is the CEO of CkR International, Inc., a billion dollar company. She is a struggling single mother working for his company in customer service. What happens during a chance meeting in his company's elevator will change their lives forever. Take the journey with Vicky and Jason as they fall in love. Will they overcome past hurts, society's demands, and family expectations?

## NEW BEGINNINGS (Out of Nowhere Series)
THIS IS BOOK TWO OF THREE

Just when billionaire Jason Kincaid Rutherford was on the cusp of living happily ever after with the only woman who's ever lit a fire within him, tragedy strikes. Will it leave her so broken that her heart doesn't have room for him? Not if Jason can help it. Continue on with the journey of Jason and Vicky as they face their biggest challenge yet.

## LOVE, LIFE, and VOWS (Out of Nowhere Series)
THIS IS BOOK THREE OF THREE

Jason and Vicky have fought hard for their relationship. They've overcome differences in culture, race, and social status. They've withstood an almost unimaginable tragedy and come out on the other side stronger than ever. Or, so they thought.

Follow along as Jason and Vicky's love is pushed to the breaking point after life takes a devastating turn. Will they ever find their happily ever after.

Printed in Great Britain
by Amazon